W9-AVK-253

Withdrawn

THE
DEVLIN
—QUICK—
MYSTERIES

SECRETS
FROM
THE
DEEP

LINDA FAIRSTEIN

**DIAL BOOKS
FOR YOUNG READERS**

Batavia Public Library
Batavia, Illinois

DIAL BOOKS FOR YOUNG READERS
PENGUIN YOUNG READERS GROUP
An imprint of Penguin Random House LLC
375 Hudson Street
New York, NY 10014

Copyright © 2018 by Linda Fairstein
Map © 2018 by Mina Chung

Penguin supports copyright. Copyright fuels creativity, encourages
diverse voices, promotes free speech, and creates a vibrant culture. Thank
you for buying an authorized edition of this book and for complying with
copyright laws by not reproducing, scanning, or distributing any part
of it in any form without permission. You are supporting writers and
allowing Penguin to continue to publish books for every reader.

Printed in the United States of America
ISBN 9780399186493

1 3 5 7 9 10 8 6 4 2

Design by Mina Chung
Text set in Chaparral Pro

This is a work of fiction. Names, characters, places, and incidents either
are the product of the author's imagination or are used fictitiously, and
any resemblance to actual persons, living or dead, businesses, companies,
events, or locales is entirely coincidental.

FOR PARKER, MATT, and ALEX,
wishing you many fish tales and
an occasional doubloon

1

"Don't go into the ocean, Dev," Booker Dibble shouted to me. "It isn't safe!"

"I'm just wading in up to my ankles for now."

"But the lifeguard isn't here yet," he said. "If there's a strong riptide, you could get pulled right out to sea."

"Three years on the Ditchley swim team," I said, "I think I can hold my own in a couple of feet of water."

It was just after nine o'clock on an already hot and humid August morning. Booker and I were on a stretch of beach called the Inkwell, in the town of Oak Bluffs on the island of Martha's Vineyard.

"You're way past the ankles. Looks more like your knobby knees are sunk already," Booker said. "Just back up and sit tight for a while. Make a sand castle. A huge one, maybe in the shape of the New York City Public Library."

Booker and I had solved our first caper at that great building. But I was ready to move on now. New adventures interested me more than looking back, and the key to our next caper was just ahead of me in the dark waters of the Atlantic Ocean.

"Maybe later," I said.

"The beach will get too crowded before very long. Now's your chance."

There had been a fierce thunderstorm the night before. The sand was churned up in the foamy water that was crashing around me and landing on the beach with more force than usual. I was trying to steady myself, stretching out both arms and balancing the large plastic bucket I was holding in my left hand.

"I just need to scoop up my sample," I said, leaning over to run the pail from side to side in the rough surf to gather sixteen ounces of water—and some of the sandy sea bottom—for my fall science project.

Everyone in my class had the same summer assignment. We each had to gather a water sample from the sea or a freshwater lake, to prove whether fish left their DNA behind when they swam through the area.

"I promise you the ocean is still going to be here when the lifeguard shows up. He's just running late."

"I know that. But part of the idea is that I'm going to collect my sample at a specific time every day. Nine o'clock. I don't want my first effort to be out of sync," I said. "I have to be consistent. All good scientists have a firm methodology, don't they?"

"Scientists don't take foolish risks," Booker said.

"Benjamin Franklin flew a kite when there was lightning right over his head. In fact, a kite with a silk string and a metal house key attached to it," I said, shaking my head at the mere thought. "That's how he proved that lightning causes an electric charge."

"Sounds like risky business," Booker said.

"You're just worried because your grandmother doesn't want anything bad to happen to me while she's in charge of our Vineyard visit. Isn't that right, Zee?"

Zee—short for Ezekiel—is Booker's eight-year-old cousin. He was sitting on a towel about ten feet from the shoreline, holding Booker's iPhone in his hands to keep it dry. He was busy playing with some game or app and just shrugged his shoulders.

I was so busy trying to show off my science skills to Booker—one of my two best friends—that when I swiveled my head to talk to him, I got knocked over by a gigantic wave. It rolled me around on the ocean floor, and I swallowed a mouthful of salt water as I came up for air.

"There's your sample for today, Dev," Booker said, laughing at me. "You've got more H_2O and seaweed in your stomach than you have in the bucket. Need a hand?"

I stood upright, planted both feet firmly in the shifting sand, and turned my back on Booker and Zee.

"Give me one more try," I said.

"You could stand right next to me and get your water for the day," Booker said. "Don't make more work for yourself than you need to."

"It's about the sand out here. It's been soaking forever, not like that dry stuff on the beach."

I was timing the sequence of the waves, sticking my right hand below the water's surface to stay still. Then I dragged the pail deep into the ocean floor and lifted it up, confident that I had collected not only a pint of water, but the muck below it. That stuff was home to snails and crabs and critters—maybe prehistoric ones—I hoped our science teacher had never seen.

I swiveled toward Booker and held up the pail in victory.

"Doing experiments is awesome," I said. "You were right about that. I feel like I'm on the verge of some really big discovery."

I walked toward Booker, almost completely out of the surf, and rested the bucket on a flat piece of sand. Then I backed out again, raised my hands over my head like I was about to dive, and flipped into the water. I held my breath with my head underwater, plowing into the waves and away from the beach. When I had gone twelve or fourteen feet, I lifted my head and stood up—neck deep—then walked toward shore, shaking myself off as I emerged from the water.

"You don't need to show off," Booker said.

"I was covered in sand," I said. "I had to do that to rinse it out of my bathing suit."

That was when I heard Zee call out a name. He was a quiet kid, and I was startled when I heard him yell.

"What did you say?" I asked him, cupping my hands around my mouth.

"Gertie!" he yelled again.

Zee had stopped playing with Booker's phone and now had his eyes glued to a spot near the end of the pier where the ferry from the mainland docked.

I turned to look in that direction and saw something break the surface of the water. If Gertie was a swimmer in trouble—with no lifeguard in sight—I knew that I could help her.

"C'mon, Booker!" I said, jumping into the waves and starting to freestyle my way into deeper water.

Out of the corner of my eye, it looked like Booker had followed me in for the rescue, but instead I felt him grab my right foot and tug me back toward the beach.

"Get out of the water," he said, with a tight grip on my leg.

"Someone needs to help that swimmer," I said, wriggling my body around to break free. But Booker dragged me back out until I sat on the sand like a beached whale.

People were getting out of their cars on the ferry line and snapping pictures of the scene below them, but no one was taking any action to make sure Gertie was okay.

"Gertie doesn't need help, Dev," Booker said, huffing and puffing from his battle to pull me onshore. "She's a really strong swimmer."

"You know her?" I asked, puzzled by his reaction to the crisis I thought was unfolding in front of our very eyes.

"Not personally, but I know who she is," Booker said. "She's a great white."

"A what?" I said, looking from his face to Zee's.

"She's a great white shark," Booker said. "Best to stay on the beach while she's in Vineyard waters."

2

The lifeguard and two police officers came running from the roadway past the three of us down to the water's edge, blowing their whistles loud enough to pierce my eardrums. I covered my ears and crunched my toes in the sand.

"Everybody out of the water!" the lifeguard shouted. He was trying to make up for his late arrival by sprinting ahead of the cops in his bare feet. "Get out now!"

They didn't have a thing to worry about on that front. There wasn't a soul anywhere near the shoreline. So many adults were shrieking and screaming that people were scrambling to get to the beach. The three of us were much more chill and curious about this tourist with the large fin. Gertie pretty much had the water and waves to herself. I've often found that grown-ups overreact to situations. They were all quite safe, on a wooden pier twenty feet above the circling shark.

"Look at her fin," I said, watching it zig and zag

through the rough currents. "It's huge. That shark must be ginormous."

Zee was standing up now. "Fifteen feet long. Three thousand five hundred pounds."

"You're just guessing about those numbers, aren't you?" I said to him. "And how do you know her name, anyway?"

Zee sat down again, cross-legged in the sand as the shark dove under the waves and cruised out of sight. Booker and I sat beside him. He had always been a shy kid, and Booker was used to speaking up for him.

"Zee's an expert on sharks," Booker said, taking his phone back. "I've got an app on here called shark tracker. It tells you where in the world every one of the tagged great whites is, 24/7."

"You taught Zee about that?"

"No way," Booker said. "Zee taught *me* everything. But I'm the one with a phone so he uses my app. Sharks are one of his obsessions. Right?"

Zee nodded.

Zee was a super-brainiac for an eight-year-old when he was interested in a subject, like the way he was about sharks. I'd spent time with him before at Booker's house, but we had never been on vacation together.

Zee had been reading since he was four years old, and

was much happier with a book in his hands than doing pretty much anything else. He kind of idolized Booker and loved to hang out with him.

"Can you bring me up to speed on sharks?" I asked him. "I hardly know anything about them."

Zee's eyes were fixed on the waves at the end of the pier, probably still searching for the shark he had spotted.

"Where'd Gertie go? How does that Inkwell app know where she is?" I asked him.

"Talk to her, dude," Booker says. "No need to be shy around Dev. She's family."

Zee looked up at me like I was the dumbest person on the beach. "There's an oceanographic institute on Cape Cod," he said.

My tongue would have tripped over all the syllables in that word when I was eight.

"The scientists there put electronic sensors on great whites," Zee said. "They tag them. You know, they kind of safely trap them for an hour or so, and then attach a little GPS to the dorsal fin."

"Ouch!"

Zee shook his head at me. "Sharks don't have nerve endings in their fins. It doesn't hurt them when they're tagged."

"Oh! Phew."

Zee punched in the app on Booker's phone. "Once that fin is above water for ninety seconds," he said, "the sensor pings, and we know where each one of these sharks is."

"What else do you know about Gertie?" I asked.

Zee cocked his head and glanced over at Booker.

"Don't worry," Booker said. "She won't tell Grandma."

Booker's parents—both doctors—had gone to Vassar College with my mother. Zee's mom was Booker's aunt, and we were all staying at their grandmother's summer cottage in Oak Bluffs.

"I won't tell her what?"

"Zee's not supposed to be using my shark tracker app," Booker said. "He's got some homework of his own to do, and it's not about fish."

"My lips are sealed, guys," I said. "I'm really curious, and I don't know anyone who knows as much as you do about sharks."

Zee smiled at the compliment.

"So the scientists think Gertie's about thirty-five years old," he said, "and they know that she likes to move around a lot. Last winter she swam all the way south to Georgia, and this summer she's been up north off the coast of Canada."

"Why?" I asked.

"She likes cool water," Zee said, "and she likes to eat seals."

"Whoa! I didn't know that," I said. "I mean about the seals."

"That's why Gertie always comes back around here in the summer," he said. "There're lots of seals that hang out on the little islands off Cape Cod, and that means they swim right past Martha's Vineyard to get there."

"So how do the great whites follow the seals?" I asked.

Zee pursed his lips and looked at me. "Sharks have an amazing sense of smell," he said. "They can sniff out a seal colony miles away."

I scanned the surface of the water for Gertie's fin, hoping there were no seals anywhere close by. I like seals way better than sharks.

"Is your elbow bleeding?" Zee asked me.

I lifted it up and brushed off some seaweed. "No. That's just an old scratch that's healed up. The scab looks red, is all."

"Good thing," he said. "A great white can smell a single drop of blood, even if it's in a billion drops of water."

I cringed. I didn't want to be anywhere near a seal colony or have a nosebleed while I was in the ocean.

The Ditchley swimming pool was beginning to look like a mighty fine place to do my laps.

"Don't go scaring Devlin," Booker said. "Check the app for us. The lifeguard's looking at his phone, too. They won't let anyone back in the water until they know where Gertie has gone."

"She hasn't come up for a few minutes," Zee said. "She's probably on her way to another beach."

The large car-ferry that brought people to Oak Bluffs from Woods Hole on Cape Cod had docked and probably forced most of the fish to scatter out of its path.

"Did you know great whites have at least three hundred teeth, Dev?" Zee asked, apparently enjoying the way he'd spooked me. "Sharp ones, shaped like little triangles, in seven or eight rows."

I pulled my knees up to my chest and wrapped my arms around them. "It's getting kind of cloudy, don't you think? Maybe it's a good day for a tennis lesson."

Zee laughed. "You are afraid, aren't you?" he said. "Booker says you aren't frightened of much."

"You got me, Zee! I'm not putting so much as my big toe in that water today," I said, standing up again with a brand-new thought. It was as though a lightbulb had gone on in my brain. "But I've got an idea for you. If you help me with my science project, I'll help you with your homework. I love to do book reviews."

He frowned. Maybe he was worried that he wouldn't be able to figure out my sixth-grade problem.

"Mine's about sharks," I said, hoping he could short-cut my science reading by telling me things I didn't know. "I'm sure you can do it."

"That's weird," Booker said. "You didn't tell me your project was about sharks on our way over to the beach a little while ago."

"That's because I didn't know you were going to introduce me to a great white," I said, my excitement growing as I thought things through. "It changes everything."

"It scared you, too," he said. "Didn't it?"

"Totally. I'll write about Gertie if you like. She'll be part of my essay," I said. "You can tell me more about her habits, and maybe I can even find out how she got her name."

Zee hesitated for a few seconds and then spoke. "I named her."

"No, really. I'm sure the people at the institute can tell me."

Zee was clicking on the app again. "There's Mary Lee,

Harvey, Vader, George, Oscar," he said, reading from the screen. "There are fifty-one tagged sharks around here. And I'm the person who gave Gertie her name."

"He did, Devlin," Booker said, taking off Zee's baseball cap and replacing it on his cousin's head, turning the bill to the back. "Zee's the man."

"That's so cool," I said. "How did you get to do that? And who did you name her for?"

"Gertie Thaw," Zee said, puffed up and proud to tell me the answer.

I screwed up my nose and gave it a quick think. "Should I know who that is? I don't think I've ever heard of her."

"I guess you don't know anything about pirates," he said.

"I know who Blackbeard was. I know that Queen Elizabeth made Sir Francis Drake one of her famous 'Sea Dogs.'"

Pirates were another of Zee's obsessions, which I sort of remembered just now when he said the word. Sea Dogs, he had told me, were raiders given permission by Queen Elizabeth I to loot the Spanish ships carrying treasure from Central America back to Spain.

Zee bowed his head and readjusted his baseball cap.

"Gertie Thaw was real, too," he said. "Lived on Mar-

- 14 -

tha's Vineyard. She was the girlfriend of a pirate who stole a lot of treasure and sailed it right here to Oak Bluffs."

"Then that's a great name for a shark," I said. "Especially a Vineyard shark."

"Do you know what an anagram is?" he asked.

"Sure I do. It's words you make by rearranging all the same letters from other words."

My math teacher used the identical example over and over to tell us what an anagram was. "Young ladies," she would say, with a satisfied grin, "a decimal point with its letters moved around spells the words 'I'm a dot in place.'" Even mathematics has its anagrams. Pretty cool, when you think about it. Exactly the same letters, all switched about.

"It's not just that she was a pirate's friend," Zee said, trying to dumb it down for me. "Gertie Thaw's an anagram, too."

"For what?" I asked. A pirate's girlfriend and a ginormous shark? I didn't get the connection.

Booker was laughing and giving his cousin two thumbs-up.

"Fifteen feet long and 3,500 pounds," Zee said. "The letters in 'Gertie Thaw' also spell the words 'great white.'"

3

Zee's two obsessions—pirates and sharks—blended into a single creature, a huge predator with hundreds of incredibly sharp teeth who had messed up my plans for a morning swim.

"Here's my idea," I said. "I'm betting that you know what DNA stands for."

"Sure I do," he said. "It stands for deoxyribonucleic acid."

Zee had gone from four syllables "oceanographic" to seven syllables "deoxyribonucleic" without missing a beat.

"It's what stores all the genetic material about living things in our cells," he said.

"Exactly," Booker said. "It's like our individual fingerprint. Even though we're related, your DNA is different from mine."

Zee looked up at Booker's face and smiled. "But the DNA would show that you're my cousin"

"You bet. There's no denying that fact."

"Here's the thing," I said. "A team of scientists who work at the same lab on Cape Cod as the guys who tagged your sharks have made an important discovery."

"What?"

"That pail of water that I was filling this morning? If I mail a container of it to the lab, they can tell me what kinds of fish were swimming right here off the Inkwell this morning. Stripers, blues, tuna . . ."

Zee glanced at me like I was telling a tall tale.

"No kidding," I said. "Think of it—it's about the DNA that's in every scale on every fish. Stuff from the fish's body that identifies its species comes off in the water."

Now he was absorbed by the idea of my experiment.

"Every girl in my class at Ditchley has to come back to school with water samples," I said. "Katie Cion is doing hers right now, out at the end of Long Island, in Montauk. Some are dunking their pails in the Hudson River or in Turtle Pond in Central Park."

"What kind of fish are in Turtle Pond?" Zee asked.

"There's largemouth bass," Booker said, "and brown bullheads. But what's really crazy is that people sometimes dump stuff from their fishbowls—you know, tropical fish from their homes—into the park ponds. Dev's friends are going to come up with some super-strange fish scales."

"We can beat that with Gertie," Zee said, jumping up next to me.

"I would have been content with stripers and blues, Zee," I said, happy to include him in my project, "but you're going to turn my science class on its head."

Zee high-fived me and looked around on the beach. "We need another pail."

"Isn't that woman in your grandmother's book club?" I asked, pointing twenty feet away. "The one over there? I'm counting two toddlers and six pails."

Zee took off in her direction, quickly talking the woman out of a bright purple bucket.

I headed toward the pedestrian walkway onto the pier. The next ferry was nowhere in sight, so I figured we had almost an hour before the cars would line up to load for the return trip to Cape Cod.

"Know any of those old guys fishing off the pier?" I asked Booker, as Zee caught up to us. "Gertie was swimming at least twenty feet below the edge of the dock. Do you think you can get some extra fishing line to tie to the handle of the bucket?"

Booker gave me two thumbs-up and came back with a line, which I double-knotted around the handle of the pail before passing the pail to Zee.

"You're my partner in this," I said to Zee. "Why don't you make the scoop?"

Zee got down on his knees and then stretched his body across the platform we were standing on. He lowered the pail, played with different angles until he got some water in it, and then looked back up at me.

"It's really deep water here," he said. "Do I have to get a lot of sand from underneath it, too?"

"No, my sand sample is good. Get as much as you can. It's mostly whatever came off Gertie's scales that we want from this spot, if we're lucky."

Zee carefully hoisted the pail up to the pier so that the water didn't slop over the sides.

"You did it!" I said. "No other kid in my class has a chance of getting shark DNA."

"No guarantees on that," Booker said. "Katie's scooping her water from the ocean, too."

"Well, not one of them will know the name of their shark if they do get it," I said, smiling at Zee, "never mind who *named* it."

We walked back to the beach to retrieve my first pail and our shoes and T-shirts. I spread a towel on the sand and took out a few clean plastic containers from my beach bag.

I dumped out the water from my earlier scoop and

took off the lid of a second container. Now there was only sand in my first pail, sand that I hoped was inhabited by lots of tiny critters.

"Hand me the strainer, please," I said to Booker.

"What strainer?"

"It's in the bag," I said. "Becca let me borrow it this morning."

Booker and Zee's grandmother, Rebecca Dylem, was called Becca by just about everyone who knew her, and she had known me since the day I was born. She once told me that when Booker started to talk, he couldn't pronounce Rebecca, so her nickname had been given to her by him.

"Can you hold the strainer really still over the specimen jar?" I asked.

I angled the pail and slowly poured its contents into the strainer, watching the grains of sand filter through the mesh. "Let's do your pa

"Whoa!" Zee said. "There's snails and teeny sand crabs and some weird-looking things with green wings. They're all plopping into the strainer."

"I'm hoping I got some rare species they've never even seen at the lab before."

I tilted the pail and poured out more sand, until it had all run through the wire mesh.

"Let's do your pail now," I said to Zee.

He passed the pail he had dunked in the water off the pier to me after I opened another clean container to pour his water into.

Carefully, I tipped Zee's bucket, aiming for the mouth of the container. Water and sand slid through the strainer into the plastic specimen bottle, with nothing else—no little creatures—of particular interest.

Suddenly, I saw a flash of something shiny roll out of the pail, bigger than any snails I had dug up earlier, and heavier, too. It bounced off the edge of the strainer and landed on the beach beside us.

"What's that?" Booker asked, reaching his hand out to touch it.

"Don't do that," I said. "It might have someone's DNA on it. You don't know how long it's been hidden in the sand."

I was so excited that my hand was shaking as I shaded my eyes. I leaned over to check out my find, but Zee was in there first. His nose was practically rubbing against the bright object.

"It's gold!" he said, loud enough for people on *Cape Cod* to hear him.

"It's what?" I asked.

"It's a gold doubloon, Dev," Zee said. "We've found

some pirate treasure right here on the Vineyard."

I looked closer and saw the raised outline of a man and woman facing each other—crowns on their heads, like a king and a queen—carved into the shiny metal.

"Sharks and pirates in the very same place, on my favorite beach, and a piece of buried treasure that I scooped up in a pail all by myself," Zee said, now on his feet, spinning around and around with his arms spread wide. "This is the best day of my entire life."

4

"Where's the police station?" I asked, not budging an inch for fear of taking my eyes off our treasure.

"The police?" Zee asked. "Why? We didn't do anything wrong."

"I think we'd better report that we found this doubloon," I said. "It must belong to someone."

"C'mon, Dev," Zee said. "There aren't any more pirates around these days. Can't we just keep it?"

"Dev's right," Booker said. "It's only fair to tell the police, in case someone lost it. I mean, lots of people collect valuable coins. Nobody is saying Blackbeard dropped it here last week."

"I need something to put it in," I said.

Zee was bummed. "How about the plastic Baggie your iPhone was in to keep it dry?"

"That won't work," I said.

"What do you mean?" Booker asked.

"You can't put evidence in plastic bags," I said, shaking my head. "If there's moisture on the coin, which there certainly is right here, the plastic just locks it inside and sometimes the police lab can't do work on the object because it gets ruined."

"Whoa," Booker said. "Who's talking about evidence? You've always got crime on your mind."

"We have to err on the side of caution," I said. "It's one of my mom's favorite rules of thumb. Always be more careful than you need to, when something important may be at stake."

My mother was a lawyer who had prosecuted crimes for years. Now she was the police commissioner of New York City, appointed by the mayor—the first woman to hold the job.

My elbows dug into the sand as I tried to get as close to the coin as I could, hoping to see the detail on the face of it.

"What's at stake?" Zee asked.

"We need to try to find the rightful owner of the doubloon, don't we?" I said. "That's only fair. You don't have any idea what it's worth, either."

"If it's hundreds of years old," Booker said, "and it's real gold, it might be worth a fortune."

I blew gently across the top of the coin. "And if it's a replica, then we'll have less to worry about."

"Can you tell who's on the coin?" Zee asked.

"Not sure. Maybe it's Ferdinand and Isabella," I said, thinking of the Spanish king and queen who had financed so many of the sailors—like Christopher Columbus— who had set off from Europe to explore the Americas.

"Get your nose out of the sand," Booker said to me. "You'll be sneezing crabs before you know it."

"See that?" I asked.

"Do I see what?"

"The red stuff that kind of looks like paint."

"I see it!" Zee said, practically butting heads with me.

"Where?" Booker asked, getting back down on his knees for a piece of the action.

"Next to Isabella's ear," I said. "There's a spot not much bigger than a freckle that's bright red."

"Whoa!" Booker said. "Guess this hasn't been in the water very long or that would have been washed away."

"Or the layers of sand protected it," I said. "What we need is a paper bag. A clean one. Paper bags can breathe, but plastic ones can't."

"Who told you that?" Zee asked.

"Sam Cody," I said. "He's the detective who helps my mom. He knows everything there is to know about being an investigator. I kind of shadow him whenever he lets me so I can learn how to be a good sleuth."

"There's a food truck right next to the ferry ticket office," Booker said, turning to run up to the sidewalk. "I'll get a small bag for you."

"Why do you want to be a sleuth?" Zee asked, still staring at the crowned heads on the coin as it gleamed in the morning sunlight.

"People sometimes do bad things to other people, Zee," I said. "You know what I mean—whether it's stealing from them or hurting them."

Zee was so smart that sometimes I had to remind myself that he was only eight, and that I shouldn't talk to him about subjects that he might not be ready for.

"Booker told me that someone killed your dad," he said.

I looked at him out of the corner of my eye. "He did?"

"Is that why you want to be a detective?" Zee asked. "Do you want to know who did it?"

"I'm kind of curious about why Booker told you that," I said. "I mean, it's true, but why would he bring that up?"

"He didn't. I asked him about it," Zee said. "I think it's sad that your father died before you were even born, like Becca says. I think it must be hard that you never knew him."

I took a deep breath, fighting back tears.

"It's very sad. You're right about that," I said. "My father had been working in Paris while my mom was pregnant with me, and he died in an explosion that killed a bunch of people. I was determined that someday I would figure out who did that and why."

"I just think it's cool the way detectives help people solve their problems, Zee," I said. "They use their brains and all kinds of skills to figure out things."

"Your dad's name was Devlin, too, wasn't it?"

That fact made me smile again. "Yup. My mom named me for him. Well, my first name anyway."

My dad's name was Devlin Atwell, and my mom is Blaine Quick. From the moment I was born, it was clear to her that she and I were going to be facing the world alone together, without my dad. So she gave me his first name, but wanted me to have her surname. The older I get, the more I appreciate having a combination of them both.

Booker came running toward us and I shook off my thoughts and got back to the work at hand. He handed me the bag.

"Where did you say the police station is?" I asked, gathering up all our gear and our specimens.

"It's across the street from the ferry ticket office,"

Booker said. "Right over there, that white building facing Ocean Park. What were you two talking about?"

"I was just about to ask Zee," I said, changing the subject as we started to walk, "how he got so interested in pirates."

"It was kind of by accident," Zee said, trying to keep up with Booker and me. We both had long legs, and Zee was pretty short for his age. I was in a hurry to get our doubloon to the local cops.

"It was more clever than that," Booker said.

I really liked how Booker was always happy to pump Zee up.

"It started with my dad's name," Zee said. "I was playing around with anagrams, and it was just like a lucky thing."

"So what is it about your dad's name? Dylem." I said it out loud three or four times as we waited for the guard to wave us across the busy road. "Luke Dylem. What's lucky about that?"

I was playing with the letters in my head but getting nowhere.

"Mud. Mud key. I know that doesn't use all of them, but am I close?" I asked. "Maybe if I had a piece of paper I could play with the letters."

"You're taking too long," Zee said. "It was so easy for me."

"It was easier for you when you were five than it is for me now at twelve," I said, crossing the street behind Booker and Zee.

"I saw my dad's name one day, written out, on an envelope—Luke Dylem," Zee said. "The letters sort of jumped right out at me."

"They did?" I said. I just couldn't see it.

"Those same letters also spell the name Lemuel Kyd."

I stopped to think for a minute as I stepped up on the curb. "You got me again, Zee. Am I supposed to recognize that name?"

His eyes opened wide as he stared at me in disbelief. "You don't know about Lemuel Kyd? He was one of the most famous pirates ever!"

"Lemuel Kyd? That's news to me."

"He's not as famous as Blackbeard, but he was a really cool sea bandit, Dev," Zee said. "I can tell you lots of stories about him. How he attacked the Spanish ships sailing home from South America with tons of gold on board, and then he came up to the New England coast to bury his treasure."

"Wait a minute," I said, stomping my foot on the sidewalk. "The pirate who buried treasure on islands all along the Northeast was Captain Kidd. But William Kidd, not Lemuel. You're just teasing me."

"He's a real person," Zee said, running in front of me and turning to face me to get my full attention. "No relation to Captain Kidd at all. Lemuel was from England, not Scotland, and he spelled his name differently. K-Y-D, not K-I-D-D. But he was an awesome pirate, too."

"If you say so," I said, shrugging my shoulders, not quite sure whether to believe Zee's story. "You know more about that than I do."

"This could be *his* treasure," Zee said, pointing to the paper bag in my hand.

"That's a long shot, isn't it?" I asked.

"It might not be as long as you think," Zee said, as Booker held the door to the police station open for us. "Lemuel Kyd is the pirate who buried all his treasure on his girlfriend's farm. On Martha's Vineyard."

I cocked my head and said, "Okay."

"And by the way, Kyd's girlfriend was Gertie Thaw."

5

"I'm Sergeant Wright. How can I help you?"

The young woman behind the desk at the Oak Bluffs police station was dressed in a navy blue uniform. She was African American, probably in her thirties, and flashed a warm smile that made us feel welcome in her office.

"I'm Devlin Quick, ma'am. These are my friends, Booker Dibble and Ezekiel Dylem."

"You're Becca's grandsons, aren't you?" the sergeant asked, looking at them.

"Yes, we are," Booker said. "Do you know her?"

"For a very long time. It's my job to know everyone in town, but your grandmother is a special lady," Wright said. "I heard she's been coming here since she was a little girl."

"Yes, she has," Booker said. "She tells stories about those long, hot drives here when she was young."

"How about you, Devlin? Are you an islander, too?"

"A different island, Sergeant," I said, smiling back at her. "I live in Manhattan. I'm just visiting with the Dibbles and the Dylems."

"Aha! You're a washashore then."

"I'm a what?"

"That's what we islanders call folks who aren't from here. You all just wash ashore, especially in the summer," Wright said with a laugh. "Now, how can I help you? You didn't get scared off the beach because of all that commotion with the shark, did you?"

"No, ma'am. I didn't exactly want to meet her any closer than we were, but we didn't let that shark get in the way of what we needed to do."

"That's good to hear," Wright said. "What was that exactly?"

I placed the paper bag on the countertop in between us.

"I needed to do a science experiment in the ocean, and Zee was helping me with it," I said. "But while we were collecting water samples, we scooped up this old piece of gold ten feet off the beach. Zee thinks it might be pirate treasure from a hundred years ago or more."

Sergeant Wright opened the bag and peered into it. She was about to reach in and lift the coin out.

"Excuse me, Sergeant, but I wonder if you might have

a pair of gloves you could put on. You know, the kind you would wear at a crime scene?"

"Look at you!" she said. "You think your buried treasure is connected to a crime, do you?"

"We don't know that, of course," I said. "That's why we brought it here to you. To see if anyone reported a valuable coin missing or stolen."

"The only items reported stolen in the last two weeks are a moped and a Yankees baseball cap," Wright said, without even looking at any paperwork. "But this island is Red Sox Nation, so I'm not too concerned about the enemy cap going missing. This is a very safe island."

"I know that," I said. "But would you mind just checking the blotter?"

"The blotter?" Wright said, raising an eyebrow.

Zee reached his hand up and tapped on the green desk blotter on the countertop. "Yeah, could you please check this?" he asked, although he didn't seem really sure about why he was asking Wright to look at it.

"That's just an ordinary desk blotter," I said to Zee. "The kind I'm talking about is slang for a book where officers make notes of thefts and things."

"You've got the police lingo down, too," Wright said to me. "You don't happen to be on the job, do you? You seem a little young for that."

Now it was my turn to smile. *On the job* was an expression police officers used to identify themselves as members of the department when they were off duty or in plain clothes. Sam Cody was always telling people he was "on the job" when he needed to help someone in trouble and he was flashing his gold detective badge.

"No, ma'am," I said. "I'm not. But my mother is."

"I like hearing that," Sergeant Wright said. "A sister in blue. Where's she a cop?"

"She's not exactly a cop," Booker said, trying to score a point with the sergeant. "Dev's mom is the police commissioner of the City of New York."

Wright looked at me and whistled. "That's awfully cool. I've seen your mother on the news. I've read a lot about her, too. She's a force to be reckoned with, isn't she?"

"That's putting it mildly," Booker said. "My aunt Blaine is a genius at solving crimes."

"Well, I don't think there's any crime to solve," the sergeant said, "but you can be sure I'm putting on my crime scene gloves. I don't want Commissioner Quick thinking we've got shoddy methods here on the island."

Wright turned around and took a pair of gloves out of a cabinet against the wall, put them on, and came back to us. She slid her hand into the paper bag and lifted out the coin, holding it carefully on its rim between two fingers.

"Whoa! This looks like the real deal," she said. "If this is gold, your college tuitions are all taken care of. I don't need a police blotter to know there's been no report involving anything this valuable."

"Really?" I asked.

"This is a small island," the sergeant said, turning to look at the back side of the large disc. "People talk. I haven't heard a whisper about anything like this. How's your hearing?"

"It's actually pretty good, Sergeant," I said.

My grandmother Lulu Atwell could hear me open the pages of a book from three rooms away if it was supposed to be lights-out and time for bed. She could tell that my dog, Asta, was sniffing at crumbs I'd dropped even after Lulu had left the table and was halfway out the door on her way to the opera. I had inherited that trait, according to my mother. My Atwell ears had helped me solve a few capers.

"I'll put some feelers out," Sergeant Wright said. "You three keep your ears open for gossip."

"How about the doubloon?" I asked.

"Seems to me that old legal principle 'finders keepers' is the law of the land, don't you think?" she said, placing the coin on the counter. "I'll just take a few photos of the piece in case anybody makes an inquiry, but you might as well hold on to it."

"Thank you very much for trusting us," I said to Sergeant Wright as she snapped some shots, then made a notation on a police report labeled Lost and Found. "But I'm not really sure that's the law."

"What do you mean?" Zee asked, ready to go for the gold and leave the police station.

"I almost forgot," Wright said, "your mother was a federal prosecutor before she became commissioner. What else could it be?"

"I think there's all kinds of laws about property found in international waters," I said. "We'll have to be very careful with this piece."

"International waters?" Wright said, pursing her lips. "I thought you said you picked this up a few feet off the beach? I'm pretty sure my Vineyard rules of thumb will do the trick."

She put the coin back into the sandy bag and handed it to me. I liked her attitude, but I know my mother is a stickler for the law.

"You wouldn't happen to be aware of any experts on the island who specialize in information about pirates?" I asked. "I mean, Zee knows an awful lot, but maybe there's someone who's been around longer?"

"There are experts in just about every subject on this island in the summertime," Wright said. "Just ask any one of them you pass on the street and they'll tell you about it themselves. Movie stars, politicians, famous authors."

"Really? Right here?"

Wright went on. "Doctors, lawyers, Wampanoag chiefs in Aquinnah. My husband is Native American, from up-island. Pick a subject, Devlin, and I'll find you an expert."

"Like I said, Sergeant, how about pirates?"

"Let me think a minute," she said. "I guess you could talk to Artie Constant, over at—"

"I know him!" Zee shouted, barely able to contain himself. "He goes way back with Becca."

My head was whipping back and forth between the sergeant and Zee. She was writing something on a blank piece of paper.

"You'll find him at the lighthouse," she said.

"Which one?" I asked. "Aren't there five lighthouses on the island?"

"Right through town and around the corner," Zee said. "Mr. Constant's at the one on East Chop."

Wright handed me the paper, and Zee practically

grabbed it out of my hand. The words written on it said EAST CHOP LIGHTHOUSE TOWER.

"If anyone knows anything about pirates or sunken treasure or shipwrecks, it's Artie Constant," Wright said. "He's been the lighthouse keeper here for half a century. I'd say Artie knows all the secrets from the deep."

"Thank you so much, Sergeant," I said, handing the slip of paper to Zee. I put our treasure inside my tote bag and zipped it closed. "If you ever need a favor in New York City, my mom's the one to call."

"Pleased to meet you," she said. "I'll hold on to that idea. Come on back if there's anything else I can do for you."

We closed the door behind us and went down the steps to the sidewalk.

Zee ran ahead of us.

"Hold up," Booker said. "Where are you going?"

"To the lighthouse."

"Don't you think we ought to drop the coin off with Grandma, so it stays safe?" Booker asked.

"There isn't time," Zee said. "Let's find Mr. Constant."

"What's your hurry?" I asked.

"Can't you see what these letters spell out?" Zee asked, waving the piece of paper at Booker and me.

"You mean the ones the sergeant wrote? East Chop Lighthouse Tower?" I said, repeating our destination out loud.

"It's an anagram, Dev," Zee shouted at me. "The words on the paper also spell a clue."

"What kind of clue?" I asked.

Zee looked at the letters one more time. He squinted for a few seconds. Then he spoke. "THAW . . . TREA-SURE . . . CLOSE . . . HIGH."

He laughed and started running again.

"Not so fast, Zee," I said. "Wait for Booker and me."

But Zee turned the corner and was out of sight before I could tell him that his spelling was all wrong.

6

"You've got to slow down with this anagram thing you do," I said to Zee. "Booker and I can't do it as fast as you can."

"It's what I do," he said. "It's what I'm good at."

"The letters in your 'Thaw treasure' words don't quite fit, Zee. We have to double-check the spelling before we're sure it's any kind of a clue."

I had convinced both Zee and Booker that we needed to stop at Becca's to show her our doubloon and leave it with her before heading off to the lighthouse.

I showed Zee the pad I had sketched the letters out on. I came up a few short with the phrase he had tried to create.

"Sometimes it takes me a few tries to get it right," Zee said.

"Nothing wrong with that. It's just that you can't rush to conclusions because you want to make pieces

of a puzzle fit, especially if you're pushing the pieces—
or in this case the letters—where they don't belong."

"We've got to take a meticulous approach to our
work," Booker said. "That's what I've learned from
teaming up with Dev."

Zee took the pad. I saw him spell out Booker's name
and then mine.

"Please don't go making an anagram with *my* name,"
I said. "Everyone comes up with the word 'devil' when
they mess with mine and nothing else that makes
sense, so I'm really kind of over that, okay?"

Zee sipped his drink and smiled. He was clearly
amused.

The three of us were sitting in rocking chairs on the
wide porch of Becca's house on Lake Street, a few blocks
from the Inkwell—the beach we had started out on this
morning. She had served up some of her homemade
lemonade and gingersnap cookies, and we were telling
her about our great find at the beach.

Becca was every bit as excited for us as we were for
ourselves. "You could even write a story for the *Gazette*
and get it published," she said.

"That's the local paper," said Zee. "We could do that
together."

"Good idea," I said.

"What do you know about Gertie Thaw?" Booker asked Becca.

"The lady or the shark?" she asked, fanning herself with a magazine to try to stir up a breeze.

"I'm leaving the shark information up to Zee," I said. "What happened to Gertie the pirate's girlfriend?"

"I may look old to you, darlin'," Becca said, chuckling at me, "but I didn't exactly know Gertie."

"Of course not. I didn't mean to be rude," I said. "But what's the island lore about her? About her family?"

Becca was seventy-five years old. She was born in Alabama, but had moved north after college and had taught school in Manhattan for almost fifty years.

Becca pulled her chair around so that we were sitting in a circle. "You all know that this island was home to Native Americans for centuries, until the British came along in the early sixteen hundreds."

"Wampanoags," I said, "like Sergeant Wright's husband."

"Exactly. They named the place *Noepe*, which means 'land amid the streams' in their language, which is also called Wampanoag."

"Who was Martha?" I asked.

"The first captain who claimed the island for the British had a daughter named Martha," she said, "and at that time, the entire place was overrun by wild grapes, so they gave it the name 'Martha's Vineyard,' for the grapes and in honor of the captain's daughter."

I loved a good history lesson, and Becca's story brought the island to life.

I pulled my chair in closer to listen.

"The first English settler to come to this island in the sixteen forties was named Thomas Mayhew," Becca said. "He was a missionary, trying to convert the Wampanoags to Christianity, and he was careful to honor their land rights."

"There are Mayhews all over this island," Booker said. "So the Native Americans were friendly to the Mayhews when they arrived?"

"Absolutely."

"What about the Thaws?" Zee asked. "When did they come? Didn't they sail on the *Mayflower*?"

"No, Ezekiel," his grandmother said, "the Thaws weren't passengers on the *Mayflower*. They didn't have that kind of money or background. There's a rumor that one of their forefathers was a master gunner on that ship, and that his grandchildren eventually settled here."

"Settled where?" I asked.

"In Chilmark," Becca said. "Janice took you there on

her island tour. It's one of the six towns on the Island. Heaven help us, but every visitor gets my daughter's three-hour tour into every nook and cranny of this place."

"Oh, yeah," I said, "it's that part of the island with all the farms."

"Chilmark is the most peaceful part of the Vineyard," she said. "No shops except the general store, no ferries, no tourists walking around dripping their ice-cream cones while they try to buy T-shirts.

"Back then, Chilmark was where the cows and sheep were raised. The Thaws had a farm spread out over an entire hilltop, up over one of the ponds."

"How about now?" Zee asked. "Do they still own the farm?"

"Over the years, the land got chopped up into smaller and smaller pieces. Each time a young Thaw married and started a family, the elders would parcel off a few acres and give them a homestead," she said. "There ended up being more Thaws than there was land."

"How about Gertie?" I asked, helping myself to another glass of lemonade.

"I'm not sure my daughter—or your mother, Dev— will appreciate my talking to you about this kind of thing," Becca said. "Ezekiel, why don't you go get those pirate coins you made me buy you at that museum on

Cape Cod. Show them to Devlin." She seemed to be trying to coax him out of the room.

Zee liked the idea. He was up and in the door in seconds.

"Gertie was a bit of a wild child, kids," Becca then said to Booker and me. "The story that's passed around is that when she was about sixteen, Lemuel Kyd and his crew had taken refuge inside the pond down below the Thaw farmland. He was running away from the Spanish fleet, after sinking a galleon off the coast of Florida. A hurricane blew in, and the pond was not only calm but out of sight from the larger ships that stayed outside, along the coastline, hoping to reach the mainland to catch up with Kyd—or at least, where they thought he had gone."

"And did he come to hide his treasure here, too?" Booker asked.

"Maybe," Becca said. "If every one of those rumors about pirates burying gold bars and coins of the realm were true, these New England islands would have sunk long ago from the weight of all that treasure."

"Did Gertie run off and become a pirate?" I asked.

"Those sea dogs didn't allow women out on the ocean. Gertie offered shelter to Lemuel and his gang on her father's property, in an old cow barn," Becca said.

"Let's just say he took advantage of the poor girl's hospitality."

"I've watched a lot of those old movies with my mom," I said. "The ones where the tough guys show up needing help, and promising to change their ways, then ride off into the sunset while their girlfriends are left to milk the cows and darn everybody's socks."

"Well, Devlin Quick, your mother and your aunt Janice and all the women like them broke that mold, you know," Becca said, laughing with me. "There'll be no darning socks for you."

"Yeah, but it sounds like Gertie Thaw got the short end of the stick," I said. "I bet she got her heart broken by that pirate."

"Could be, but I've told you all I know," Becca said. "When you get old enough, you can research the story and write a book about it."

"Maybe there's already a book in the local library about the story. Mom's always encouraging me to expand my horizons by reading books that teach me things."

"Blaine's always been a bit ahead of the curve in that regard," Becca said. "I'd still be pushing *Rebecca of Sunnybrook Farm* as your reading material. What makes you so interested in my storytelling today?"

"Here's this pirate doubloon," I said. "What if it actually belongs to the Thaws?"

"This coin is a really mysterious thing," Booker said. "If we can figure out who it belongs to and how it got here, we'd be doing something good for the people who lost it."

Zee came rushing back out onto the porch, carrying a black suede pouch with a long string tie.

"Did Gertie ever get married?" I asked. "Did she have any children?"

"No to both questions," Becca said. "That's what I've been told."

"But there were a lot more descendants in the Thaw family, weren't there?" Booker asked. "Are any of them still out on the property in Chilmark?"

I knew what my partner in crime was thinking. What if there was buried treasure from the time Lemuel Kyd had hidden in Gertie's cow barn?

"There are Thaws here and about," Becca said. "They sold off that old farm a few years back. Some film producer from Hollywood bought it and started to put up a mega-mansion. But there doesn't ever seem to be anyone there and I'm not sure the building was ever completed."

Booker looked at me and winked. Maybe a visit to the

old Thaw homestead would be a fun adventure. Maybe there were more doubloons to be found!

Zee had dumped his bag of pirate booty on the porch. There were fifteen or twenty coins, most of them the size of the doubloon we'd found on the beach. Some of his treasure was the color of silver, and some pieces were a mixture of silver and bands of gold.

I kneeled down to touch them as Zee spread them out on the deck.

"Where did you get these?" I asked. "They look almost good enough to be real."

"Aren't they cool?" Zee said, squealing with excitement.

"Keep your voice down, young man. Everybody passing by will think I'm harboring a pirate," his grandmother said, teasing.

"They're reproductions," Booker said. "Feel how much lighter they are than our doubloon."

I picked up four of Zee's coins and held them in one hand, with the paper bag in my other hand. Those four didn't even equal the weight of our one antique piece.

"Becca bought them for me at the shop at the Whydah Museum on the Cape."

"That's true. I certainly did," she said.

"What's the Whydah Museum?" I asked.

"The *Whydah* was a slave ship out of Africa in the eighteenth century, built to carry slaves to the Caribbean," Becca said. "On its way back across the Atlantic, a buccaneer known as Black Sam raided the ship, freed the remaining slaves, and took over the galleon as a pirate ship. The *Whydah* sank not far from here, close to Cape Cod, and there's a wonderful museum named for it that I've taken Zee to see."

"That's a really great collection," I said to Zee, getting to my feet. "You're lucky to have it."

He was absorbed in the coins now, ordering them in a single line from the edge of the porch down the steps to the sidewalk.

"You better hang on to those," Booker said. "Don't be showing off that you have all these coins. People on the street might think they're real."

"That's what I want them to think," Zee said, raising his voice again. "They're real coins and I'm a real pirate!"

Several passersby, on their way to the Inkwell with beach chairs and umbrellas, picked up their heads when they heard Zee shout. Becca just waved at them and smiled.

"Why don't you go for a bike ride?" she asked.

The island had amazing bike trails that kept you off

the roadway, parallel to the ocean and alongside the pond where older kids paddleboarded and kitesailed.

"Good idea," Booker said. "Will you hold on to our treasure?"

"Your doubloon will be my responsibility," Becca said, taking the crumpled bag from me. "Do you mind if I throw away the bag?"

I practically gasped. "Please don't do that!" I said. "It's all part of the experiment, so I'll need to keep it. Even the bag is evidence, now. And you can't touch the coin without gloves, Becca. I mean, in case we need to have scientists perform DNA tests on it."

Becca was headed for the screen door. "Your treasure is safe with me."

Zee was scrambling to get his coins back in the bag. "How about me?" he asked. "Can I come, too?"

"Of course you can," I said. "But leave your coins at home."

Zee followed Becca to the door, held it open, and threw his bag of make-believe doubloons onto the living room sofa.

Booker walked to the garage and opened the door. There was a bike rack with six ten-speeds for family and friends to use, and a shorter one that belonged to Zee.

"Let's go toward Edgartown," he said. "There's a

hot-dog stand near the pond, so we can watch the guys sail for a while until it's time for lunch."

"How can you even think about food?" I asked, pointing my handlebars in the opposite direction. "Why don't we go to the lighthouse now?"

"The lighthouse?" Booker said, groaning as he spoke. He was hungrier than he was curious.

Zee was with me. I knew he would be.

"Let's find Artie Constant," I said, pumping my pedals and letting the wind carry my words back to Booker. "If there are secrets to be told, he's the man who knows them all."

7

I let Zee lead the way, zipping around the edge of Ocean Park, past the police station, and then cruising by the marina, full of sail- and motorboats. He made a right turn at the small market and then the tall white lighthouse—surrounded by a well-tended area of grass and flowers—came into view.

We dismounted and parked our bikes in a rack near the entrance.

There was a large painted sign announcing our location: EAST CHOP LIGHTHOUSE. 1878.

"Wow. This place is really old," Booker said.

"Unfortunately, it was built long after Lemuel Kyd was around," I said, turning to Zee. "How do we find Mr. Constant?"

There was a NO TRESPASSING sign on the front door, with a notice that visitors were welcome every Sunday from 6–9 p.m. Adults have something about liking to see the sun set, I guess, and take pictures of it. It seems to be an activity they've got to do wherever they go.

"There's a back entrance," Zee said.

We followed him around the base of the lighthouse and stopped at a narrow panel that hardly looked wide enough to be a door.

Zee had been here before. That was obvious. He pulled up on the old metal handle and pushed in. Booker and I followed him over the threshold and into the dark base of the old structure.

"Mr. Constant?" Zee called out. "Artie?"

There was the sound of footsteps coming from way above our heads. I craned my neck to look up.

"Who goes there?" a deep voice grumbled at us.

"It's me, sir, Ezekiel Lydem."

"Ahoy, matey! Been missing you, Zee," Constant said. "Climb on up here, son, and let's have a look out at the ocean. See if we've got any scallywags coming ashore."

"I've got my cousin Booker with me, okay?" Zee said, putting his hand on the banister and his foot on the first step. "And a friend of ours, too. A girl."

"Why did you have to say *that*?" I asked. "It makes no difference at all."

Zee shrugged. "Artie thinks girls are afraid of pirates."

"That is so ridiculous," I said. "Was Gertie Thaw afraid of Lemuel Kyd? Obviously not. Here we are centuries later. What have I got to be afraid of? And by the way, there are no pirates around here today."

"I keep telling you that Dev isn't afraid of much," Booker said. "Rattlesnakes and scorpions, sure."

He was thinking about my dinosaur dig in Montana last month.

"Come on, all of you," Artie Constant said.

I glanced up again. The staircase was spiral-shaped, and it wound around and around again, as the steps got narrower and narrower. I couldn't even see the platform where Artie must have been standing, it was so far above our heads. The tower was four or five stories high, and the only things inside it were hundreds of steps.

"Why don't you ask him to come down," I whispered to Zee.

"Because he's up there," Zee said. "You can practically see France from the top of the tower. What's the point of being in the lighthouse if you can't see all the ships?"

Booker started to laugh. "I forgot about heights," he said. "Dev's kinda skittish about heights, too."

"I thought you said she isn't afraid—" Zee started to say, turning to look at Booker.

"Of almost anything," Booker said. "I forgot the almost."

"Who have you brought to me?" Constant bellowed from above. "Your words echo up here, son. Seems like you have a lily-livered lass with you today."

"That's a low blow," I said, putting my hand on the thin banister.

I thought of my grandmother Lulu's advice, whenever she tried to get me over my personal stumbling blocks. *Tackle your fear straight on,* she would say to me. *The only way to build courage is to look your fears in the eye.*

I tilted my head and looked up at the top of the tower. "Cover my back, Booker, will you?"

Zee turned to face me from the step above. "What does Artie mean about your liver? Are you sick?"

I kept my voice low and leaned into his ear. "It means he's trying to bully me, just for being a girl. Back in the Middle Ages, people believed that your liver was the source of courage. Lulu told me that after I read the expression in *Macbeth*. And if your liver was the color of a lily—you know, real pale and light—then it meant you were a coward."

"Louder!" Constant said. "I couldn't hear that."

I kept a tight hold on the banister and took the lead from Zee. "I'm a lass all right, Mr. Constant, but you'll be walking the plank if you have anything nasty to say to me when I reach your hideaway."

I raced up the twisty staircase, keeping my eyes focused on the spotlight at the top of the building, on the inside. I never looked down. I didn't want to think about how I would get out of this place when we were ready to go.

"Well then," Artie Constant said, reaching out to take my hand and help me onto the circular platform that ringed the inside of the tower. "You were quick for a landlubber, weren't you?"

"I *am* Quick. Devlin Quick, sir. Nice to meet you."

"Any friend of Zee's is a friend of mine," Constant said as Zee burst past me and immediately went to press his nose against one of the windows.

"I'm Booker Dibble. Zee's cousin," Booker said.

Artie Constant rubbed his hands together and talked to Zee. "So why have you brought these sprogs to me?"

"Sprogs?" I asked, anticipating another insult.

"Calm down now, young lady," Constant said. "It's just captain's talk for new recruits."

"Look, sir," I said. "I enjoyed reading *Treasure Island* as much as the next kid, but do we have to talk like sea dogs the whole time?"

Artie Constant laughed and leaned back against the iron railing. "Some of the guests like me to do that," he said. "And Zee? Well, there must be some pirate blood in his veins. It's just part of the game we play when he's up here, scanning the horizon for any ships flying the Jolly Roger."

"Pretty spectacular spot you've got up here," Booker said, moving next to Zee to take in the view.

I shivered. It must have been quite a sight, in the old days, to see a skull and crossbones on a black flag flying high above the main deck of a ship—a sure sign of pirates approaching the Oak Bluffs harbor.

"Sergeant Wright suggested that you might be able to answer some questions for us," I said. "She told us you're an expert on pirates."

Constant had thick white hair and a gray beard— a short one, but still messy enough that it looked as though a small bird could have nested in it. He pulled at the end of it while he answered me.

"I can't really be an expert in anything, Devlin," he said, picking up his telescope and moving toward one of the windows. "I grew up in this town but never even finished high school."

"My mom's got a law degree and Booker's parents are both doctors," I said, "but they don't know the first thing about pirates. You probably know more than anyone on the Vineyard, the sergeant said. In my book, that makes you an expert."

That remark seemed to please Artie Constant.

"Buccaneers and buried treasure," he said. "I've been fascinated by both them things since I was Zee's age. Maybe younger. If you think I can help you, then fire away with your questions."

"Is it true that Lemuel Kyd came to Martha's Vineyard to escape the Spanish ships that were trying to capture him?"

"That's the lore that came down over the ages," he said, "and I've got no reason to doubt it."

"Was there any proof of his visit here?"

Constant put down his scope and tugged at his beard again. "Proof? Like you mean the kind that could hold up in a court of law?"

"That would be really cool to have."

He shook his head from side to side. "Can't say that I saw any of that, hard as I looked for it."

"Tell us what you looked for," I said.

Zee and Booker turned their heads to listen.

"Do you know about the first Captain Kidd?" Constant asked. "The more famous one? He was a Scotsman, named William."

"Sure we do," Booker said. "But what became of him?"

Zee jumped right in. "The British finally got him,"

he said. "Took him to England and hung him from the gallows."

I reached for my neck and rubbed it.

"There's your expert," Constant said, pointing at Zee. "Best student I ever had."

"So when did Lemuel Kyd come along?" I asked. "I never heard of him until today."

"Much later," he said. "More than a century after William Kidd. Lemuel was English, and his country came against us in the War of 1812. Pirates were everywhere along the coast of the young United States then."

"He was a copycat pirate," Zee said. "He wanted to be just like the first Captain Kidd, getting rich, hiding his money along the New England coast—"

"Probably looking for what the first Captain Kidd left along the way, at the very same time, in typical pirate fashion," Constant said.

"—and maybe looking for a rich wife," Zee went on. "Maybe like Gertie Thaw."

"Gertie wasn't rich, laddie," Constant said to Zee, reaching out and putting a hand on his shoulder.

"Becca says the Thaws were land rich," Zee said.

"Lemuel Kyd didn't want land, matey," Constant said, picking up his telescope again and extending it to its limit. "Didn't have any use for it, except to put some gold and jewels under it until the coast was clear. Remember those pirates had stolen silks and calicoes, too, and rum from the Indies. They had plenty on board to barter with."

"Did you ever believe there was treasure here, Mr. Constant?" Booker asked. "Did you ever dig for it?"

"Most surely I did."

"Where, exactly?"

Constant's belly shook as he laughed again. "Between just about every rock that the tip of a shovel could fit. There was a time in my youth, kids—almost eighty years ago, before there were mopeds and fast cars and jet planes coming to the Vineyard—that you could walk from one end of the island, in Edgartown, to the top of the great red clay cliffs in Gayhead."

"Gayhead is called Aquinnah now," Zee said. "It's the Wampanoag word for 'high places.'"

"My buddies and I carried our shovels into every cove and scrambled over every rock formation on the coast, and we always came up dry."

"That doesn't mean that pirates weren't here," Zee said.

"You're right about that, too, laddie. Could be he sent some other buccaneers to bring it home, or that others got to the treasure before we did."

"How about Gertie Thaw's farm?" I asked.

I was forming a picture of her now: a bold girl in her new calico dress with scarlet silk ribbons, things Lemuel Kyd had given to her in exchange for a hiding place away from the ocean side of the island. Maybe he even let her have a piece or two of gold so she would keep his secrets.

Artie Constant whistled and tapped the lens of the scope against the side of his head. "I took my chances as a kid, missy, but I never went up against old Travis Thaw."

"What do you mean?" Booker asked. "How was Travis related to Gertie?"

"Gertie Thaw was one of six kids," Constant said. "Boys, all of them, except for her. Travis was the grandson who inherited the old farm. The original farm, with the hay barn where Lemuel was supposed to have hidden."

"You knew him?" Booker asked. "Did you ever talk to him about Lemuel Kyd?"

"You know how Travis Thaw talked?" Constant asked. "Only one way he communicated with anyone outside his family. He talked with his shotgun."

Zee got the drift. "He didn't want any of you coming on his land, did he? He didn't want any of you digging for buried treasure."

"Rumor had it Travis believed the stories about Lemuel," Constant said. "He used to brag about things he had seen. Maybe what you mean by proof, missy."

"Like what?" I asked.

"Like Lemuel's initials carved into wooden beams in the barn."

"Anyone could have done that," I said, beginning to feel discouraged.

"And pieces of eight. Travis claimed to have pieces of eight."

"What's the difference between pieces of eight and a doubloon, Zee?" I asked.

"That's easy," he said. "Basic pirate factoid. Doubloons were usually made of solid gold, like ours is."

I saw Artie Constant twitch when Zee said the words "like ours."

"Pieces of eight were silver dollars," Zee went on. "It took eight of them to equal the value of a doubloon."

"Whatever became of Travis Thaw's silver coins?" Booker asked. "Did anyone else ever see them?"

Artie Constant raised the telescope to his right eye and aimed it out the window.

"What's this about a doubloon, Ezekiel? Are you holding out on me, matey?" he said, ignoring Booker's question about the Thaw pieces of eight.

Before I could put my finger up to my lips, Zee answered. "We just found it this morning, Artie. In ten feet of water, right off the pier where the ferry docks."

"Let's have a look at it, laddie," the old man said, holding out his free hand. This time he wasn't laughing.

"We didn't bring it with us," he said. "Becca's holding it for us."

"Very smart of her," Constant said as he leaned in toward the window even closer. "I'll tell you something right up your alley, kids."

"What?" Zee asked.

"Come stand beside me," Constant said. "There's a small boat headed for the marina, just up the road. Take a look through my spyglass."

Zee grabbed the long telescope, stood back from the window, and took aim in the direction Artie Constant pointed him.

"See it, matey?"

Zee nodded.

"It's a stinkpot," Constant said.

"It smells?" Booker asked.

"No, my son. Boats with motors aren't as elegant as sailboats. That's just how they're known by real sailors," Constant said. "Twenty-eight-footer. Dark blue hull and white cabin. She's called *Revenge*."

"Named for Lemuel Kyd's ship, isn't she?" Zee asked, squinting his other eye.

"Well done. Indeed she might be," Constant said. "Owned by a man from New York City who came up here looking for treasure, too."

"Are you helping him?" Booker asked.

"He's a little too slippery for my taste. I sent him over to Tarpaulin Cove on the Elizabeth Islands, seven miles across the Sound. He'll find nothing but sheep over there," Constant said, "or else he owes me a pretty penny for directing him. After all, I've looked over every rock on *that* deserted island over the years, too."

Zee was following the boat into the harbor.

"Keep your eye on him, Ezekiel," Constant said, winking at me. "Don't want anybody getting our gold, do we? We're partners in this."

Zee was silent, but that didn't necessarily mean he hadn't made an earlier plan with Artie Constant, weeks ago, if they were playing around with the idea of a treasure hunt.

"What's his name?" I asked. "The man who owns the *Revenge*."

My mom's detectives could run a background check on him if he turned out to be up to no good. Maybe *he* had something to do with our coin.

"He's Cole. Cole Bagby. Has a house in Chilmark but he likes to keep his boat down here in Oak Bluffs on account of the golf course is nearby."

Zee lowered the telescope. "The *Revenge* entered the port, Artie. She's out of sight."

"You're a good man," Constant said. "Tell you what."

Zee handed the scope back to the old caretaker.

"Why don't you go home and get me that doubloon, son? Maybe I can help you to authenticate it. Maybe there's an image of it in one of my pirate books."

Zee looked over at Booker before he answered. "Sure thing, Artie."

"Bring it back before sunset. Before the tourists pile in up here."

"Thank you for your time, Mr. Constant," I said. "Zee won't get back here with it this afternoon, but we'll try to bring it by tomorrow or Thursday."

"But—?"

"Booker and I have some surprise outings planned for Zee. We'll get it up to you just as soon as we can."

"Sometimes those doubloons wind up in Davy Jones's locker, if you're not real careful with them," Constant said. "And that would be a very bad thing now, wouldn't it?"

Davy Jones's locker. The bottom of the sea. I felt a chill run up and down my spine when Constant looked at Zee and spoke those words. I knew that Davy Jones was a made-up character who ruled over the evil spirit of the underwater world, the place of shipwrecks and people lost at sea.

"No need to be rude to Zee," I said, grabbing the boy's hand and leading him to the top of the winding staircase. "You'll see the doubloon."

"I'd never be rude to my mate, now would I, Ezekiel?" Artie Constant said, holding his belly as he laughed again, only this time it sounded sinister. "Zee said the doubloon came from out of these Vineyard waters. Well, maybe that's where it belongs."

I hadn't given the first thought to the idea that my scientific experiment might have been causing some kind of disruption of calm island life. But Artie Constant's tone was menacing.

The old man waved a gnarled finger at me to make his point. "Don't put it past old Lemuel Kyd to place a curse on you for disturbing it."

8

Zee scampered down the lighthouse steps, clearly unafraid of the great height from our landing to the floor below.

Booker stayed a step or two ahead of me, knowing that this kind of descent wasn't my favorite part of the experience.

The idea that our buried treasure might come with a curse stopped me in my tracks, eight steps down and about 256 to go.

"What kind of curse are you talking about?" I called up to Artie Constant.

"Don't pay any attention to that at all, missy. It was just something squiffy that popped out of my mouth," Constant said. "I'll keep an eye on you all. You won't be having any trouble."

"Much as I appreciate that, sir," I said, "I don't want to lead my friends into an adventure that's tangled up in an ancient curse."

"You might have thought of that before you started mining for gold," he said.

"I didn't have the least interest in gold," I said. "It never occurred to me there was treasure on Inkwell Beach. I was just doing my science experiment."

The winding loops of the wrought-iron railing made me dizzy as I stared down at them from my perch. I gripped the banister and closed my eyes. My feet seemed almost glued in place.

"Tell me the truth, Mr. Constant," I called up to him. "Was anyone else cursed by Kyd?"

He paused for a minute. "It's hard to know where to start, missy. There's all those poor folk he robbed and wrecked on the high seas."

"Yes, but that's what pirates did. I mean, was anyone on the Vineyard cursed by his treasure, not just by his actions?" I reached out to grab Booker's hand to steady myself, cracking one eye open to move closer down the steps to him.

"Gertie Thaw," Constant said. "Island folks thought she was cursed all right. If she got anything valuable from Lemuel Kyd, she never shared it with anybody. She used to stand at the top of the Gayhead Cliffs on the coldest, wettest nights, letting the wind howl around her, hoping to see the *Revenge* round the bend and come back into her quiet harbor. Those silk hair ribbons he gave her were tattered to shreds."

"What else?" I asked.

"You'd have to ask Gertie's relatives about the rest," Constant said. "Hard to separate the truth from the rumors."

"How would I find them?" I asked, taking another dozen steps. "The relatives."

"Still a couple of Thaws in Chilmark," Constant said. "Then there's Jenny. Has a little house over in the Campground, near the Tabernacle. Zee's grandma knows where it's at."

"Where's the Campground?" I asked Booker.

"Here in Oak Bluffs. We can walk to it from Becca's, that's how close it is. In fact tomorrow is Grand Illumination Night. We'll be going there anyway," Booker said.

"What's Illumination Night?" I asked, speeding up my steps so I could keep a firm grasp of Booker's hand as he made his way around and around and down.

"It's an old tradition on the Vineyard," Booker replied. "Like for more than a century. I'll let Becca explain it to you."

"Some even say that the people who bought the Thaws' land carry the curse," Constant said, his voice booming overhead.

Booker looked at me and mouthed the words instead of speaking them. "Don't listen to him, Dev. Artie Constant's just trying to scare you."

"He's doing a good job," I said. The steps were getting wider on the lower half of the staircase and my footing felt steadier.

Zee was fidgeting below us, probably just anxious to get on his way. There were a number of barrels lined up against the wall next to the door, and he was opening their lids, peering into them.

"Leave them dirty old things be, mate," Constant shouted out to him. "And you, missy, there was a guy who was walking along one of the Chilmark beaches carrying a metal detector all summer, maybe ten years back."

"What do you mean by a metal detector?"

Booker answered. "You've seen people with them on the beach. They look like long sticks with a magnetized plate on the end that sucks up metal things from the sand. You know, like quarters and dimes and—"

"And every now and then a piece of buried treasure," Constant called out. "Every once in a while a doubloon."

"Really?" Booker asked. "People have found doubloons on Vineyard beaches?"

"This one old bloke claimed he did," Constant said.

"Next day, along came a hurricane, and he didn't heed any of the warnings to get off the shore, greedy as he was to find more pirate treasure. Before anyone ever saw the fool's piece of gold, the poor fellow got caught in a riptide and was swept out to sea."

I pounded down the steps as fast as I could.

"I'd call that a curse, Devlin Quick," Constant said. "Wouldn't you?"

"We get your point," Booker said. "We'll be back to show you our doubloon."

"Very sensible, laddie. I know pirate ways, and I can help you navigate around the trouble once we know exactly what your treasure is," Constant said, leaning over the topmost railing to look at the three of us. "Now you, Ezekiel, you're going to wind up a mess. What will your granny have to say?"

Zee had been peeking inside the large barrels. He withdrew his arm from the barrel closest to the door and I could see he was covered in bright white paint up to his elbow.

It didn't seem to bother Zee at all, but Booker ran the rest of the way down, picked up a cloth from the floor, and wiped off Zee's arm.

"I'm so sorry, Mr. Constant. We didn't mean to disturb anything," I said.

"Not a worry, missy. It's just time for me to repaint the old lighthouse."

I had turned my head to talk to him and wound up stumbling off the remaining steps to the lighthouse floor, bumping against the last barrel in the row. It teetered and splattered my T-shirt with red paint before it stopped rocking and leveled off.

"Are you all right, missy?" Constant asked, chuckling this time. "Just save me enough of that fire engine red color to put a coat or two on the front door."

"Let's go, Booker," I said, twisting the heavy doorknob and opening the door. "I'm covered in paint now, too, just like Zee. You'd think old Artie Constant put a curse on each of us."

I didn't realize how our voices echoed through the empty lighthouse, all the way up to the platform from which Artie watched us.

"That paint will wash right out, Devlin," he said. "Curses last forever."

9

"I hope that's not blood all over you," Becca said as we marched up the steps to her porch. "You're really a sight, Devlin Quick. I'll need some smelling salts before I call your mother to tell her about this."

"I'm so sorry to give you a fright—it's just paint," I said. "I was so clumsy I tripped over a barrel of the stuff."

"Do you still have your bathing suit on underneath?"

"I do."

"Then strip off that T-shirt and shorts right here so I can run the laundry," she said, opening the screen door. "I'll bring you some clean clothes."

"Thanks, Becca," I called after her.

The three of us sat down in rocking chairs, drawn into a circle.

"We need a plan," I said.

"Why?" Zee asked.

"Detectives always have a plan," I said. "That's how

they solve mysteries. They do things in logical order and put the clues together."

"First we take our treasure to Artie Constant," Zee said. "That's a plan."

Booker looked at me over Zee's head. "But not the first step, pal."

"Why?"

"Nothing against your friend Artie," I said. "We're just better off gathering as much information as we can before we present it to him."

I wanted to stay as far away from Artie's curses as possible. No need to rouse up any old evil spirits that still lurked around on the Vineyard.

"Why?"

Just twenty-four hours with Zee and I knew that was his favorite question. Maybe it's the reason he knew so much.

"I'm thinking that tomorrow the three of us take a ride up to Chilmark to explore the old Thaw farm property," I said.

Sam Cody always told me that getting the lay of the land was an important piece of understanding a mystery.

"That's a long bike ride," Zee said. "The hills get really steep out there, and the bike paths stop before that."

"There's a public bus," Booker said. "We could get passes and ride out early, poke around, and still be back by early afternoon. But why?"

"I'm really curious to see where Gertie Thaw lived," I said, "and to check out the harbor where Lemuel Kyd hid his ship from the British sailors."

"Dev's so good at digging that she and our friend Katie even found dinosaur fossils in Montana last month," Booker said. "Who knows what she'll turn up on Thaw land?"

"Real fossils?" Zee asked.

"Totally real. Seventy million years old," I said. "I'll show them to you when you come back to New York after the summer."

"Deal."

"So we agree on step two of the plan," I said.

"Slow down," Booker said. "What happened to step one?"

"The plan is obviously a work in progress," I said, tapping the side of my head. "Step one should be a trip to the courthouse before we head up to Chilmark. We can check the land deeds to see how the Thaw property was split up, and maybe that will lead us to the owner of the doubloon. We should find out who inherited the barn where Lemuel Kyd hid out."

"Cool," Zee said. "Is that allowed?"

"Public records," I said. "First thing tomorrow morning. We don't even need a subpoena, although my mom could probably get us one through Sergeant Wright."

"You're on fire," Booker said.

"Then, in the evening, Becca can show us where Jenny Thaw lives, in the Campground."

Booker swallowed hard. "Lulu is a great co-conspirator for you, but Becca goes by the book. She's not such a free spirit."

"Aw, she'll introduce us," I said. "Becca is so into history and family genealogy she'll be happy to put us together with one of Gertie's relatives."

"I hope you're right."

"When do we take our doubloon to show it to Artie?" Zee asked.

"How about the day after tomorrow?" I asked. "Isn't that a good plan?"

Becca pushed open the screen door. She had my clean clothes and some napkins tucked under her arm and was carrying a fresh pitcher of lemonade.

"Plan for what?" she asked. "Booker, go in and fetch the sandwiches I made from the kitchen table. Y'all must be hungry by now."

"To show our treasure to Artie," Zee said.

Becca laughed as she sponged some paint off my nose and forehead with one of the napkins she had brought out. "You know what a town crier is?"

Zee wrinkled his nose. "Like a kid who cries all the time?"

"Nothing like that," I said. "Back in colonial times, before there was the Internet—"

"How about before there were radios or televisions or telephones," Becca said.

"That, too. Well, each town had a guy whose job it was to stand in the main square and ring his bell to get people's attention to tell them the news," I said.

"It would have been Artie way back then, and it's still the way Artie acts now. Showing Artie your gold doubloon is like making an announcement to all the good folks of Oak Bluffs," Becca said. "I'll have to get a safe to keep your treasure in. Artie's my dear old friend, but he does have a big mouth."

Zee didn't seem to care, but Booker did. He liked sleuthing every bit as much as I did, and he had soaked up all the tips that Sam Cody taught us.

Booker put the platter of sandwiches on the wicker table and we each grabbed one to eat.

"How about a swim after you digest your lunch?" Becca asked.

Booker reached for his phone and clicked on the shark tracker app.

"I was thinking the same thing," I said. "Where's Gertie now?"

"Way off, near Cape Cod."

Zee nibbled at his ham and cheese sandwich. "Great whites cruise at about one and a half miles an hour. That's a fact. Cape Cod is seven miles away."

"You have more shark info than anyone I know," I said.

"They can migrate across the Atlantic Ocean," Zee said. "Thousands of miles."

"Cape Cod will do for today," I said. "If Gertie got that far away, I'm ready to dive in the ocean."

"Be sure and grab a towel," Becca said. "It's hot enough for me to take a dip, too."

"That will be fun," I said. "And just imagine if what we scooped up today had DNA from shark scales."

"Wrong again, Dev," Zee said, munching on a brownie.

"But even you said—"

"Sharks don't have scales," Zee said. "They have denticles."

"Tentacles? Did I hear you say tentacles?" I said. "Squid have tentacles, but sharks certainly don't."

Zee gave Booker a look and rolled his eyes. I'm sure he thought I was hopeless about great whites.

"I said denticles, Dev. With a *D*. Sharkskin is made of denticles," he said. "Instead of scales, sharks have these tiny V-shaped designs on their bodies that let them go faster underwater."

"Just like the fabric on the bathing suits Olympic swimmers wear," Booker said. "Probably your swim team has them, too, and you've never noticed."

"It's the same idea, guys," I said. "There's still likely to be DNA on whatever came off Gertie's back and into the water."

"But what if you don't get any DNA from our samples?" Zee asked.

"We've got bigger fish to fry," I said. "We've got the mystery of the doubloon to solve before everyone in town tries to claim it as his own."

10

I helped Becca clean up after lunch, waited for her to put on a bathing suit, and then the four of us set off, with Booker carrying a beach chair for his grandmother over his shoulder. He and Zee were making tracks faster than Becca could walk.

"How old were you when you started coming to Martha's Vineyard?" I asked her as we crossed the road to stay on the shady side.

"I was just a baby," she said. "Been coming here summers all my life, and my mother's family long before that."

"Why to this place? Tuskegee's a long way from here."

"What do you see when you look around, Dev?"

"It's the most beautiful island I've ever seen. The beaches, the stone walls, the farms and the fancy houses, too. I get that."

"What else? C'mon, you're smarter than that."

"The people?"

"The island is very special," Becca said, "and its diversity is part of its great attraction for me. The Vineyard's got a long history of celebrating African American culture, especially here in Oak Bluffs."

"How did the Inkwell get its name?" I asked.

We were crossing the street, making our way around Ocean Park with the sand just over the horizon. The old Victorian houses that ringed the park were framed by the pale blue and green flowers of scores of hydrangea plants, and the sun was sparkling on top of the water. I was searching the beach for Booker and Zee.

"Well, things have certainly changed," Becca said. "Most of the African Americans who came here all that time ago settled in this town. On a hot day in summer, the beach would be crowded with black people. It was others—white residents and tourists—who said this beach looked like an inkwell, and they didn't mean that as a compliment."

"Boy, that was mean!"

"I can laugh at it now, Dev, because we've made that name our own. Point of pride, if you will. Now the Inkwell is known worldwide. I can say to my friends in Chicago or San Francisco or even in Paris, 'I'll meet you at the Inkwell next July,' and they'll know right where to find me."

I smiled at her as we waited for two tour buses to pass by.

"You'd better put strong sunscreen on, young lady. You're likely to fry."

"I've got some in my bag," I said, thinking about what Becca had said.

By the time we spotted Booker and Zee, they were waiting for us at the edge of the shore. Booker had set up Becca's chair and our towels in the middle of the beach.

The scene was much more relaxed than it had been in the morning. The beach was crowded now, just like Booker had said it would be. There may have been a few more lifeguards than usual, but nobody seemed the least bit afraid to be playing or swimming.

"Go ahead," Becca said. "Booker and Zee are waiting for you."

I dropped my bag and took off my T-shirt, rubbed lotion, all over myself and ran to the water's edge. Zee had his boogie board, and we were each so happy to be able to go in to swim that we barely noticed how cold the Vineyard water was. "Bracing," as Lulu liked to call New England temperatures.

At five o'clock, Becca told us to gather our things so she could go back to the house to make dinner.

"Can we take Dev to the Flying Horses?" Zee asked.

"I don't see why not," his grandmother said. "But be home by six."

"What are the Flying Horses?" I asked.

"It's the oldest carousel in America," Zee said.

"You went there with me years ago, when we were just little kids," Booker said. "You used to love it."

"I can barely remember it," I said. "Of course I want to go."

"It's just three minutes from here, right in the middle of town," Booker said.

Becca said she was fine to carry the light aluminum chair back to the house. She gave Booker money for a few rides and told us she'd see us at home.

The brown wooden frame of the old building was so ordinary looking that you'd never know it held such a magical ride inside.

There were six or seven kids sitting astride the wooden horses, younger ones held in place by a parent standing beside them, and older ones happy to be galloping around to the cheerful calliope music.

"Twenty horses," Booker said. "Take your pick."

When the machine came to a stop and the riders dismounted, Zee ran straight for his favorite pony. It was a palomino, with a bejeweled saddle and bright eyes.

He stopped to stroke the long tail of his animal. "It's real horsehair, Dev," he said. "So is the mane."

"Need a boost?" Booker asked.

"I can do it myself," Zee said, standing on tiptoes.

His pony was on the outside row of horses. "See that metal arm, Dev?" he asked me. "That holds the brass rings. And if you grab one on your way around, you get a free ride."

"I'll be on the pony right behind you," I said.

Booker took the horse next to Zee, on the inside track. Each pony was a different color, and each had been lovingly painted and restored.

The music started up and the giant engine beneath the carousel platform roared to life, moving the entire field of ponies around, slowly at first and then faster and faster.

I wondered if I was too old to admit how much fun it was to be back on a flying horse. Everyone around us was laughing and playing with their reins and shouting encouragement to their horses.

There were so many happy sounds that I couldn't hear the three boys—about my age, I guessed—who were waiting in line for the next ride and yelling something in our direction.

We circled around twice and each time we got near

their position they cupped their mouths and called out something again.

I thought they were trying to talk to Booker, or maybe to Zee, but as good as my hearing is, I couldn't make out their words.

Then I noticed that Zee had stopped reaching for the brass ring as the carousel continued spinning. He was sitting back in his saddle, almost still.

I saw Booker balance himself and swing his left leg out of the stirrup, walking around Zee's pony and standing between his cousin and the edge of the moving platform.

"Booker!" I said. "What's happening?"

And then my chestnut stallion neared the trio of rowdy boys, and this time, I could hear their words clearly.

I held on tight to the horn of my saddle and copied Booker's dismount, running ahead to stand next to Zee. I pulled out my iPhone and turned on the video camera, to capture the three guys and record their cruel words.

I put my arm around Zee's back, but when I looked up at his face, I saw that his smile had faded and his eyes had filled with tears.

"*Cray-Zee, Cray-Zee, Cray-Zee.*" The three bullies shouted the word and chanted in unison.

"Ignore them," Booker said.

But that was impossible to do.

"Hey, Zee," the leader of the pack called out, laughing as he did. "Did you know that you're *crazy*, dude? Nobody who isn't crazy reads as much as you do."

11

The carousel was beginning to slow down.

Booker and I surrounded Zee, ready to help him dismount.

"Here's the deal, cuz," Booker said. "Nobody's going to hurt you when Dev and I are around. And we're going to help you learn to stand up for yourself."

The bullies had no weapons—only words—but it was clear just how much their words hurt.

"You ready to tell these creeps to cut it out?" Booker said.

Zee didn't speak. His short legs barely reached the stirrups and he had to hold on to the saddle and slide down the pony's side.

"I know it's hard for you to do," I said. "We know they're much bigger than you are, but Booker and I will be right next to you."

"The guy at the front of the line goes to my school. I'm pretty sure his name is Levi," Booker said. "He's picked on you for the last time. You're going to look him right in the eye."

"He scares me," Zee said, reaching for my hand.

I grasped it and held it in mine. "We're here for you. Can you tell Levi to stop?" I asked. "Tell him to stop calling you names."

"Be strong," Booker said. "We know you can do it. We won't let go of you."

"No, I can't. I can't do it," Zee said. "I bet nobody ever made fun of *you*."

"Are you kidding?" I said. "That's why I can help you. Teenage boys make fun of how skinny I am all the time. And if I lose a swim race at school, the other team's swimmers taunt me about my name. They like to tease when I'm too slow—just because my name is Quick."

Zee wiped his nose and looked up at me. "Really?"

Booker not so much. He was one of the coolest guys in school. But he'd always stood up for friends who'd been bullied.

"You're the smartest guy I know," I said. There must be a way he could show these punks that his big brain was an awesome thing to have.

The flying horses ground to a stop. We were only a few feet away from Levi and his bully-buddies, who showed no sign of backing off.

Zee was frozen in place.

"I know you from Hunter High School," Booker said, turning toward the trio. "You're Levi, aren't you?"

"So what? So what if I am."

"Zee here is my cousin," Booker said. He had one hand on Zee's shoulder and the other on the long brass post at the edge of the platform. "There's nothing crazy about him. What's wrong with reading a lot? That's nothing to make fun of."

"You've picked on Zee for the last time," I said, not sure Booker and I had the means to stop them.

Then Zee said something to me.

"What?" I leaned in and asked.

"That kid in the middle—the one behind Levi—he was on that boat that Artie Constant sent off looking for treasure today. That stinkpot."

"How do you know?" I said. "Are you sure?"

"Yes, I saw him through the telescope. He had that same striped T-shirt on, and the marina is just around the corner from here."

"Good detective work, Zee."

"C'mon, Zee," Booker said, as people were clearing the carousel for the next riders to get on. "Tell Levi it's over."

I squeezed Zee's hand. "Go for it. We're going to turn the tables on them."

Zee took a deep breath and spoke. "I want you to stop. Stop making fun of me."

Levi had probably never heard Zee talk. He was looking back and forth between Zee's face and Booker's.

"Good job, Zee," I said to him, under my breath. Then I had an idea. "Now take Booker's phone, and open the shark app."

He squeezed me back before letting go of my hand and reaching for Booker's iPhone.

Booker looked at me and raised his eyebrows. "What are you doing, Dev?"

"What's your last name, Levi? Unless you're afraid to tell me! After all, I'm at Ditchley, and I could out you to my classmates as the biggest jerk at Hunter when we get back to school next month."

"You don't scare me one bit," he said. "My name is Levi Harts. What's the difference?"

"No big deal," I said. "Just checking you out."

Levi folded his arms and snickered at me.

"Got a sister?" I asked him.

"No sibs," he said, laughing at me.

"How about you, in the back?" I said. "I could hear you shouting something nasty at Zee a few minutes ago, so why don't you tell me who you are, so I can keep track of you, too?"

"I'm Emil," he said. "What of it?"

I wanted their names just in case they did anything to hurt Zee in the next few days. I wanted them to think I was keeping tabs on them, as Sam Cody liked to say.

"C'mon, Levi," the kid in the middle said, acting real fidgety. "Let's go get something to eat."

The three of them turned their backs to us and started to walk.

"Mr. Bagby," I said. "What's your hurry?"

All three stopped in their tracks.

"How do you know my name?" Bagby asked. "I don't go to Hunter. You can't know me from there."

"*Revenge* seems like a pretty perfect name for a boat owned by someone like you," I said.

He seemed really spooked that I knew who he was *and* that he had a boat.

"What's your first name?" Booker asked.

The kid hesitated.

"Ross. My name is Ross."

"So *you're* the one with a little sister," I said. "She was on the boat with you this morning."

All three of the guys looked stunned.

"Where is she now?" I asked.

"Now?"

"Right this minute," I said. "Is she here on the Vineyard?"

Ross Bagby looked back and forth between his buddies and me. "Why do you want to know?"

"Is she at Tarpaulin Cove?" I asked. "Or out on State Beach?"

"You can't touch her," Levi said, standing up for his friend. "She's on the Cape this afternoon. In Chatham."

"Go on, Zee," I said.

Zee's fingers moved over the shark tracker app faster than I could say Chatham Beach. "Any sign of Gertie?" I asked.

Zee shook his head. "Nope, she's over near Hyannis."

"C'mon, Ross. They're talking nonsense," Levi said.

"Got anything?" I asked Zee.

"Well," he said, standing up as tall as he could, "I hope your sister isn't swimming right now."

"What's it to you?" Ross asked.

"'Cause there's a great white shark named Hercules that's circling the beach over there," Zee said. "And his friend Moby is just a few feet behind him."

Ross Bagby was frozen in place. "But how—how do *you* know?"

"C'mon," Levi said. "The kid's just pulling your leg."

"There are three hundred fifty species of sharks in

the ocean," Zee said, exuding confidence about something he knew better than anyone. "And two really huge great whites are munching on anything kicking around on Chatham Beach."

Levi and Emil started to run off. Ross followed, digging his phone out of his pocket. "Wait up, guys. I have to call my mom. She's got to get those girls out of the water."

"Don't forget to thank Zee next time you see him," I called after them. "Walk back your mean words, why don't you?"

"And you ought to watch out when you're over at Tarpaulin Cove," Zee shouted to Ross, feeling empowered. "Great whites really like it over there. Pirates often buried their treasure at places sharks liked to hunt, 'cause it frightened other people away."

I could see that Ross's hand was trembling as he tried to speed-dial his mom.

I grabbed Booker and Zee and hugged them both at once.

"Your knowledge is power, Zee," I said. "Don't ever forget that."

Zee high-fived me and started to skip away from the carousel. He had taken on one of his greatest fears and come out stronger than ever.

12

"Is that really true about Tarpaulin Cove?" I asked, trying to distract Zee until the bullies were out of sight.

"Yup," Zee said. "'Buccaneer Banks' is what they used to call the caves and coves where pirates hid things. Sharks, they figured, would keep treasure hunters away."

"Hey, buddy," Booker said. "You rocked this just now. You made me so proud to be your cousin."

Zee looked at Booker and smiled. "I could only do it because you and Dev were with me."

"I don't believe that," I said. "I bet you've known all along that you could handle bullies."

"Let's go tell Becca," Booker said. "Think how happy you'll make her."

"What's your favorite ice-cream flavor?" I asked.

"Mint chocolate chip, of course," Zee said, starting to sprint in the direction of the house.

"After dinner, we can walk to Mad Martha's," I said, "and I'll treat you to a double scoop with sprinkles."

"For being a shark expert?" he said, stopping to look back at me.

"For being brave," I said.

He turned to put his head down and kept jogging along.

Booker was as relieved as I was. "Good idea you had about Zee's superior shark sense," he said. "I guess I won't ever call you a skinny geek again."

"Better not," I said, laughing with him. "And how about an apology for all those jokes you made about me when my braces were on?"

"If I apologize for that, will you buy *me* an ice-cream cone, too?" Booker asked.

"Not yet. I've got to go through the whole list of things you've said to make fun of me. Twelve years' worth. I'm not letting you off that easily."

"Twelve years? Don't be ridiculous. I couldn't even talk for the first eighteen months of my life. And then you were a pretty cool toddler," Booker said. "Before you grew up to be the way you are. Actually, it's just been a year or two of me goofing on you."

I ignored Booker and played back the video on my phone. "Look at this. I got the whole event on film. If these guys ever act nasty again, I've got ammunition to show their parents."

When we arrived at Becca's, Zee was waiting for us on the porch. He held the screen door open and we went inside.

"What's for dinner, Becca?" Booker asked.

She called out from the kitchen. "I'm grilling up some striped bass, caught right in Vineyard Sound this morning," she said. "Corn on the cob, grown on the island, and tomatoes from my backyard garden. Will you kids set the table?"

"Happy to," I said.

"We've got dessert covered," Booker said.

"What? You don't like my blueberry pie all of a sudden?"

We were all in the kitchen now. Becca was seasoning the fish and watching over the pot of boiling water for the corn.

"Everybody loves your pie," I said. "It's just that I promised to take Zee out to Mad Martha's tonight."

"He's a lucky kid, isn't he?"

"C'mon, Zee, tell your grandmother what a great thing you just did."

Zee stared at the fish.

"Zee?" Becca said. "C'mon, now."

Zee told her about the carousel ride and the bullies. She bit her lip when he got to the part about the name-calling.

Then Zee pulled himself up and stood straight, repeating to his grandmother what he had said and done.

She wiped her hands on her apron and pulled the eight-year-old tight against her. She buried her face in the top of his head, and I could have sworn she was shedding a tear or two that she didn't want Booker or me to see.

"You've got a strength in you that you didn't even know you had," she said, picking up her knife again. "Every one of us does, when we finally figure out how to use it."

"It was Booker and Dev," Zee started to say.

"It was entirely you, Ezekiel," his big cousin said. "End of story."

Zee grabbed the silverware and helped me place it on the kitchen table.

"Well, it sounds like you had a more productive hour than I did," Becca said.

"Why?" Zee asked.

"Artie Constant came knocking on my door, on his break from the lighthouse tours. You just missed him by a few minutes."

"Was he looking for me?" Zee asked, still anxious to show off our treasure.

"No, sir. Seems Artie's still got a little spark in him yet," she said, chuckling while she talked. "He wanted to know if I'd go to the Tabernacle with him for the sing tomorrow, for Illumination Night."

Booker practically doubled over. "Artie asked you out on a date? That's funny."

Becca turned and picked up her wooden spoon, shaking it in Booker's direction. "Don't you be rude, Booker Dibble. I'd be a fine date—just maybe not for Artie."

"Lulu has dates all the time," I said. "She really thinks she's the life of the party, Becca. And I mean *every* party."

"Yeah, but that last guy who took Lulu to the opera dropped dead on her," Booker said. "Don't you remember that?"

"Yes," I said. "But Lulu claimed it was the bad music that got him, not her company."

"So what did you say to Artie?" Booker asked.

"I said no. The four of us are going together tomorrow night," Becca said. "I told him it was a family event. I don't have you all here for very long, and I don't need to share you with Artie Constant."

"That's very nice of you," I said.

"Besides," Becca said, getting ready to go out back to grill our fish, "I'm not really sure if it's me or your gold doubloon old Artie was aiming to see."

13

"What have we got here?" the town clerk in the public records office said to us as we stood in front of his counter at eight thirty on Wednesday, the next morning. "Early birds trying to snatch the worm? I'm just opening up for the day."

Booker introduced the three of us and told the clerk that he and Zee were Becca's grandsons. Her name seemed to unlock every door on the island.

"I'm Harry Mason," the clerk said. "What is it you're looking for?"

"Do the property records come with maps?" I asked.

"Some do." Harry scratched his head. "Early ones mostly, because there were a lot of people who couldn't write very well, but could draw the boundaries of their property."

"We'd like to look at some of the old deeds from up in Chilmark," Booker said, giving the man his most sincere Dibble-dazzle smile. "Kind of trace one family's history as it came down on the island."

"Ah, yes," Harry said. "There are some assignments you just can't do on the Internet. It's probably what keeps me in business. Any family in particular?"

I tried to be casual about my interest. We didn't need anyone else to think the three of us were looking for buried treasure. "People who've been here a really long time," I said. "Like the Thaws. Becca says there aren't so many families left."

"Thaws it is," Harry said. "That will be twenty dollars."

"Twenty dollars?" I said. It never occurred to me we'd have to pay to see public records. "Is there a discount for law enforcement?"

Harry laughed. "Don't tell me you're the new sheriff in town?"

Zee giggled, too. He was waiting for us near the door.

I was tempted to tell Mr. Mason about my blue and gold detective shield from the NYPD, our reward for the case Booker and I had worked on in June, but my mother made me leave it at home in the city.

"No, sir," I said. "It's just that I've got a relative who works for the police."

"I'm sure you're very proud of him," Harry said, "but—"

"Her. I'm very proud of her."

"Understood," he said, holding out his hand. "It will still be twenty dollars."

Booker pulled me aside. "I've got the money for the bus passes that Becca gave me, and twenty more for the rest of the day. What have you got?"

"Fifteen, all together. How about we skip lunch?"

"We can all share one lobster roll," Booker said, returning to the counter to hand Mr. Mason his twenty.

Harry opened his drawer to put the money in. "Do you want to start in the seventeen hundreds?"

"The eighteen hundreds will be fine," I said. That was the time of Lemuel Kyd's visit.

"Sit yourselves down at that big table and I'll be back with the record book."

I took out my pencil and notepad. Sam Cody made it clear to me ages ago that detectives always have a notepad handy. It was dangerous to trust important details to one's memory.

Harry returned with a gigantic book, a volume the size of my school desktop bound in red leather that had started to crack and fade.

"Town of Chilmark, 1800–1899," he said, placing it on the table between Booker and me. "Happy hunting. Lucky for you, this end of the island was mostly fishermen and merchants. Chilmark was the farming area, so there were much larger parcels of land with fewer houses on them and even less property transfers."

"Where do you think we should start our search?" Booker asked.

"The original big Thaw homestead was way out past Beetlebung Corner," Harry said.

Some of the place names on this island really made me laugh. Beetlebung, Booker had told me, was a mix of two old English words—*beetle*, or the mallet that was used to hammer wood in the old days, and *bung*, for the pieces of wood that were pounded together to make barrels to hold oil onboard whaling ships. The two main roads in Chilmark crossed each other at Beetlebung Corner.

"Look for references to the Thaws on the south side of Menemsha Pond," Harry went on.

"Me-nem-sha?" I repeated. "Is that a Wampanoag word?"

"Exactly so, and it means 'still waters,'" Harry said. "It's a nice calm pond that feeds out into Vineyard Sound."

"Is the pond away from the ocean?" I asked.

"Yes, indeed," Harry said, walking back to the counter and leaving the three of us to our search.

"Did you hear what he said?" I whispered to Booker and Zee. "A pond on the Thaw farm! It sounds exactly like the right place for Lemuel Kyd to have pulled in from the Vineyard Sound to avoid the British sailors who were after him. I'm already thinking about more doubloons!"

"Exactly," Booker said. "You're a faster reader than I am, Dev. Why don't you start turning pages?"

"How about me?" Zee asked.

I pushed my pad and pencil over to him. "Take notes, okay? That's really key. And here's my phone, so you can snap some photos of the pages."

Original records and land deeds had been bound into this enormous book. The pages were yellowed with age, but thick and sturdy.

I started turning pages and reading family names aloud. "So far we've got Davis and Solon and O'Hayer properties," I said. "Each one has hundreds of acres."

"They were really huge farms in those days," Booker said. "Some of them are still pretty large."

"Thaw!" I said, stabbing the page with my finger. "Here's one. Jared Thaw."

Booker leaned in and Zee poised the pencil to start writing.

"Wrong guy," Booker said. "Our Thaws lived on the pond, not on the Atlantic side of the state road. You can see the piece of land on the map."

The next few pages were different views of the same property, drawn by hand, with the names of the farmers who bordered the large parcel.

Harry Mason must have heard us talking. "I'm sure I can help you. I've been through these books dozens of times."

"That would be great," Booker said.

Harry came over to our table and used his forefinger to guide us across the road, to the Travis Thaw property.

"It's pretty simple," Harry said. "Travis Thaw, Jr., had a brother named Jared. Once Travis had a wife and three kids in his house, he needed to move Jared out. Sold all this land across the road to Jared for the sum of fifty dollars."

I was practically crawling into the big book to follow Harry's story as he flipped through the deeds and maps.

"Eighteen fourteen. It doesn't look like Travis Thaw bought any more land, but he must have had another child," Harry said. "He's adding a name to the rightful heirs, this says. And he built a new structure on the property."

"Travis Thaw, Junior, and Madeline Thaw—and their issue," I read, over Harry's shoulder.

"What issue?" Zee asked.

"It's a legal word that means kids, Zee. I've heard my mom use it."

Booker was reading along with me, and Zee was listing the names on my pad. "Travis the Third, Zachary, Franklin, Bartholomew, and Gertrude. Two more kids than they had when they sold the piece to Jared."

"And then a new baby a month earlier," Harry said, "named Benjamin."

The second page showed that the Thaw farm was bounded on the north by the shore of Menemsha Pond, on the west—separated by a stone wall—by a farm owned by the Denman family, on the south by the old highway now known as State Road, and on the east by a small inlet called Lovey's Cove. One set of neighbors, and three natural boundaries.

"Lovey's Cove?" Booker asked. "That's an odd name, too."

My eyes were scanning the page. "Aunt Lovey—looks like that's her actual name—was one of the Thaw's ancestors."

"She got a cove named for her," Booker said. "More than Gertie got."

"Gertie got a shark," Zee said. "I'd rather have a shark with my name than a piece of dirt."

"A cove," I said. "A cove in a corner of a very calm pond, which happens to be out of sight of the ocean—safe from British sailors and the fury of a hurricane."

"Could be the place where Gertie met the pirates," Booker said.

I turned and curtsied to him. "Lemuel Kyd, I'd like you to meet Gertie Thaw."

"I doubt you curtsy to a pirate."

"I bet my Gertie would use all her skills to get Lemuel to hang out in her neighborhood for a while, gold doubloons or not," I said. "Must have been pretty bleak out there with five brothers and not many other people around."

"I guess you're right about that," Booker said. "Let's put our heads together and see if we can Thaw this out." Zee and I laughed.

We thanked Harry for his help, and then Zee walked to the opposite side of the table, leaning over to look at the drawings on the second page of the Thaw property records.

Booker and I were shoulder to shoulder. "There's room for you, Zee. You don't have to try to figure this out upside down. That's so much harder."

"I like it this way. I'm good upside down."

Booker put his finger on the large building that was

closest to us. It was the biggest structure on the huge spread of land.

"This is the farmhouse," he said. "It's closest to the main road."

"How can you tell?" Zee asked.

"That's how they built in those days. So they had easy access to the roads."

"Then there are these paths that go to the bodies of water," I said. "This wide one leads downhill to Menemsha Pond, and this narrow one goes from the main house down to the side here, to Lovey's Cove.

"The wide one is kind of exposed," I said, drawing an imaginary circle around the large pond. "Anyone living on this pond could see pirates coming and going."

Zee had the perspective from the far side of the pond. "But if Lemuel Kyd tucked his boat from Vineyard Sound through the pond and into that little cove at the far end of the pond, just below the side of the house, why he'd practically be out of sight to most of the neighbors."

"Now you're thinking," Booker said.

"What are these structures?" I asked.

"There's a barn next to the house," Booker said. "It's marked 'Wagon.'"

"What's that big thing?" I asked, squinting to try to see the drawing.

"The cow barn," he said. "That's how it's marked. 'Cows.'"

"Looks practically as big as the house," I said. "Doesn't it?"

"The Thaws were farmers, Dev. They had a herd of cows."

"There's another building behind the cow barn," I said. "Half as big as the barn, but I can't read the words."

"I can," Zee said, even though the tiny lettering was upside down. "It says 'camp.' But why would the Thaws have a camp?"

"That's another one of those things that happens to language over time," Booker said. "Camps were kind of temporary housing structures, not places for kids to go in the summertime, Zee. Soldiers put up camps, and Becca told me a lot of farmers used to build makeshift camps so extra workmen had places to sleep when they were hired to help with raising animals."

My excitement was growing. "Maybe it was a pirate camp."

"Don't get ahead of yourself, Dev," Booker said. "Sam

always tells you to follow the facts, not to drag them along the way *you* want them to go. Neither Becca nor Artie Constant mentioned anything about Lemuel Kyd hiding out in a camp on the Thaw property. They talked about the cow barn."

He dragged his finger to the large structure on his left that was clearly marked for cows.

"Sort of weird," I said. "That cow barn is too far away from the water, where Kyd's boat would have been anchored."

"How about *this* barn over here?" Zee asked.

He pointed to a sketch of a building that was way down the hill from the main house.

"It's marked 'sheep,'" Zee said. "It's a sheep barn."

I put my finger right on the spot that was Lovey's Cove. "I like it, Zee. Say Kyd's boat, the *Revenge*, is anchored right here."

Then I slid my finger over the ridge, stopping right at the sheep barn. "It's a pretty clear path from the cove to the sheep barn, and more likely that Gertie had a reason to spend time with the sheep," I said. "Getting the wool to do her darning and her knitting, especially when Lemuel was around."

"Not baaaaaaaaad, Dev," Booker said, imitating the bleating of a sheep. "Not bad at all. Here we've been looking for a cow barn, when maybe all along Lemuel Kyd was counting sheep at the same time he was counting his gold doubloons."

"Let's give this back to Harry," Booker said, closing the heavy volume. "It's time to get our noses out of the books and snoop around the old Thaw homestead."

Zee hesitated. "But, isn't that trespassing?" he asked.

"Why, Ezekiel Dylem," I said, "you know there's proper, professional sleuthing in my very DNA. Booker and I aren't about to break the law. My mother would have me grounded for the rest of the summer."

Zee ran ahead and pushed open the door.

I looked at Booker and raised my hands, palms up. "Nancy Drew, Miss Marple, Sherlock Holmes—each one of them trespassed to solve a case. Am I right?"

"I know they're your idols, Dev, but they're fictional," Booker said.

"But they're real sleuths in the pages of good books," I said. "Honestly, is there a better detective than Sherlock Holmes that ever existed?"

"How about Commissioner Blaine Quick?" Booker asked. "Look, we're flesh and blood. And we don't have any connections to the Chilmark Police Department. So let's start by going to the Thaw farmhouse and knocking on the front door, just to keep us legiti-mate."

"But I thought your grandmother said the house is kind of deserted."

"Well," Booker said, "we'll just have to cross that cove when we get to it."

14

The bus driver pulled over to the side of the road at the crest of the hill after the wide overlook that offered a spectacular view of Menemsha Pond and the Vineyard Sound beyond it. Once I saw how high the hills were on this end of the island, I understood why we couldn't have biked out here.

"The old Thaw property is your second driveway on the right," the driver said. "Walk straight in till you see the house with three white chimneys."

"Thanks very much," I said to him. It was only ten thirty in the morning, but the sun was hot and I could smell the salty ocean air, not far from where we stood. "Let's go, guys."

I trudged up past the first driveway. There was a hand-painted white sign that said TURNBULL WAY PRIVATE PROPERTY. I looked down the neatly mown path but couldn't see any houses before the bend in the road.

Fifty feet later we came to TRAVIS LANE. I stopped in

the middle of the graveled drive and waited for Booker and Zee. "This way in," I said. "And there's no mention of private property, like the other road, and there's not a NO TRESPASSING sign."

Zee reached for Booker's hand. His green plastic pail and shovel, which I had encouraged him to bring in case we picked up any more treasure, hung from his other hand.

We walked for four or five minutes before the house came into view. The overgrown shrubs on the side of the road led all the way up to the old stone wall that separated the driveway from the path into the house. The beach rosebushes were dead and the plantings that probably once had been vibrant colors were wilted and splayed on top of the browned-out grass.

I quickened my pace and headed for the front door of the old farmhouse. It didn't look like parts of it were as old as others I'd seen, but it now sat abandoned on this isolated hilltop.

I took two steps up and lifted the brass door knocker, which still had the THAW name inscribed on it. Even before I knocked, I was pretty certain no one would answer. There were no cars next to the house, and no sign of life around it.

I tried the knob but the door didn't open.

"Are we trespassing yet?" Zee asked. I knew if he got too nervous he would start to freak out. I would, too.

"Nope. Just looking for the owner."

I stepped down and peered through the glass into a window. It was what my mother liked to call a "great room," a large living space with a huge fireplace on one end and lots of sofas and chairs inside.

"That's what's left of the cow barn," Booker called out. "Just that broken-down old wooden frame."

I followed Booker and Zee off to the left, to the once-tall building that had housed the Thaw herd. The roof was still held up by the original walls, and part of the hayloft was supported by solid old beams. But I bet it had been a long time since any cows had slept there.

Booker walked ahead of me, rounding behind the house as he scrolled through the photographs Zee had taken of the deeds in the record books.

"Wait until you see this view," he said. "It's pretty amazing."

The Thaw property was in a perfect spot. From its unusual height, you could see all the land that sloped down to the pond, the entirety of the pond across to the actual village of Menemsha, and then beyond Vine-yard Sound to the Elizabeth Islands. On a sunny day like this, it looked as if you could see forever.

Zee walked back to stand on the deck, which was clearly a recent addition, with its barbecue grill and a fire pit surrounded by lounging chairs.

"Down below!" Zee yelled. "Someone has been digging up the land."

Booker and I jogged down the slope, in the direction of the pond.

"Nothing sinister, Zee," he called back. "Looks just about the size of a swimming pool."

"Artie did say that some Hollywood producer bought this place from the Thaws, started to fix it up, and never came back," I said.

Zee saw his opportunity and seized it. He went flying down the hill, got down on his knees and began shoveling the earth that had already been loosened and moved by the workers who had started construction on the pool.

"Hey, Zee," I called out, "what are you up to?"

"The construction workers made it easy for me to dig right here," he said. "Who knows what I'll find?"

"I like your thinking," I said.

Booker was studying his photographs, turning his phone in all angles. "I don't see any sign of the camp. Do you?"

It should have been somewhere between the cow

barn and the stone wall that separated the property from the Denman farm, which I could see in the distance.

"All gone," I said.

"And it looks like that stand of cedar trees on the top of that ridge below Zee is hiding whatever is left of the sheep barn, right?"

"I think so," I said. "You stay here with Zee. I'm going to walk from the sheep barn around to Lovey's Cove, and then back here to the porch behind the house. I'll be out of sight for a few minutes, but I want to see where a pirate might find a secret hiding place."

"Okay, I'll take some photographs."

I went to the bottom of the hill, below the pool area, then climbed up the ridge, with the house at my back.

The sheep barn was still there but hidden from sight of the farmhouse because it was at the bottom of a steep incline. I ran toward it and had to catch my breath when I landed smack up against it.

Unlike the other buildings, it was in fine condition. It had been rebuilt and the trim around the barn door and windows was painted in a gray-blue color that suited the old country look of the structure.

I pulled at the door but it didn't open. I stood on tiptoes and looked in the window. It had been redesigned as an office. There was a long table in front of the window, facing the pond, but nothing on it—no books, no lamp, no papers.

Now my imagination had taken hold. I walked back from the door of the sheep barn, making my way over tree stumps, avoiding the poison ivy branches as I walked, and winding up with one foot on the shoreline and the other in a couple of inches of water.

For a few minutes, I was young Gertie Thaw, my heart pounding in my chest, making my way around the point of land that jutted into the pond and led me directly to Lovey's Cove. I could almost see the Jolly Roger blowing in the breeze, and I was overjoyed that the *Revenge* and its crew had navigated their way into the secret landing that would give them safe haven on the property.

The only thing that interrupted my few minutes of make-believe was the sound of a siren. I lifted my head and saw the flashing red light of a police car at the top of the hill, pulling up to the front door of the old Thaw farmhouse. Not only was my chest pounding, but my knees were shaking badly, too.

15

"It's my fault, Officer," I said, panting after running uphill and circling the house, to find the Chilmark cop standing over Zee. "Not his."

"Are you digging for trouble, son?" the khaki-uniformed officer asked.

Zee was kind of frozen in place, his shovel in his hand, sitting cross-legged in the giant hole that was supposed to become a swimming pool.

"I did that once, sir," I said. "Never again."

"What's that, young lady?"

"Zee doesn't mean any trouble, sir," I said. No need to tell the officer about my fossil dig in Montana. *That* was trouble. "It was all my idea to come up here."

Booker was walking up from the pond, where he had gone to take pictures. I waved to try to hurry him up.

"Are we trespassing?" Zee asked. He was pretty agitated, so I put my arm around his shoulders. "Are you going to arrest us?"

The officer scratched his chin. The plastic tag pinned to his shirt showed that his last name was Brewer.

"Normally, I'd have to think you were trespassing," Officer Brewer said, "but this hunk of land is for sale, son, so the owner has been encouraging everyone in town to send folks up to look it over. Would you like to buy an old farm?"

We each breathed a huge sigh of relief—about the law, not about the sale. "My allowance won't stretch that far," I said.

"Mine either," Officer Brewer said. "Mrs. Denman's the neighbor who saw you from her kitchen window and called over to the station. She said there was some unusual activity here."

"We didn't do anything unusual officer," I said. "We're very law-abiding. Zee—well, all three of us—have this thing about pirates, and we were coming up to the old Thaw farm to see if we could look at the cove where Lemuel Kyd hid from the Spanish."

"We even knocked on the front door to ask if the owner would mind if we walked around," Booker said.

"You didn't go in the house, did you?" he asked.

"No, sir. We'd never do that," I said. My hands were behind my back and I crossed my fingers on both of them. If the front door hadn't been locked, who knows what I would have done to try and get to the bottom of the mystery of the doubloon?

"Then there was nothing for Mrs. Denman to worry about," Brewer said. "The owner is some kind of big deal in the movie business, which does not make him a big deal in Chilmark at all. The house is completely empty, so I'm not sure why she worries so much whenever she sees movement on this hilltop."

"Then it's okay if we poke around?" Booker asked.

The officer put his hands on his hips and shook his head. Whenever my mother took that position, I knew it was time to move on from whatever I was doing.

"I'd say your poking is done for the day," Brewer said. "Get your young friend to take his pail and shovel to the beach for the afternoon. There haven't been any pirates sighted on this pond in a couple of hundred years."

"That doesn't mean there isn't any more buried treasure," Zee said.

"Move along, son," Brewer said. "There's more pirate booty at the Inkwell than there is on this place. You ought to go down to Oak Bluffs."

Booker and I both turned our heads to look at the officer.

"Excuse me, sir," I said. "Did you mean there's pirate treasure at the beach?"

"That's the word at the police station," he said. "Heard it this morning from one of my fellow officers who lives in Oak Bluffs. The story's all over town."

Zee was up on one knee. "That must be my—"

Booker grabbed Zee's shoulder faster than I could blurt out "don't say it."

"Must be your imagination, cuz. Let's get moving."

Zee was standing up between Booker and me. "But I'm hungry now. I don't want to go to the beach."

"Are you three staying up here in Chilmark?"

"No, sir," Booker said. "But my grandmother gave us money to buy lunch at Larsen's Fish Market. Can we walk there from here?"

Officer Brewer pointed his finger. "Larsen's is in Menemsha, that small village directly across the pond. Due north, if you swim. A lot longer on foot. But it will only take me five minutes to drive you there."

None of us were happy to leave the Thaw farm, but we didn't have a choice.

"You ride up front with me, son," Brewer said to Zee, smiling at him and trying to put him at ease. "I bet you've never been in a police car before."

Booker looked at me and winked as we climbed into the rear seat. Courtesy of my mother and her job, the two of us had been in dozens of NYPD RMP's—radio motor patrol cars—the way some kids are spoiled by using Uber. And we'd ridden with Sam Cody and my mother in the commissioner's spiffy black SUV, lights flashing and sirens blaring, more times than I could count.

"This is cool," Zee said, taking in all the police equipment on the dashboard.

Officer Brewer made a U-turn and headed back to State Road, explaining to Zee what each one of the devices did.

"Curses," I whispered to Booker. "Foiled again."

"I think it's the villain who says that line in old cartoons."

"Well, we're the good guys, but I am feeling foiled."

The road wound and turned and we went downhill and up again, past the Chilmark General Store, through Beetlebung Corner, and around the bend to the tiny fishing village of Menemsha.

Officer Brewer stopped his car in front of Larsen's Fish Market, a cool looking gray-shingled building that sat right on the harbor.

"You kids know your way back to town?"

"Yes, sir," I said. "We've got bus passes."

"Good," he said. "The bus stops right there, in front of the Texaco station, and comes about every twenty minutes."

Booker opened the door and I slid over and got out.

"Remember," Brewer said, "there's no point snooping around the Thaw property till you save your pennies—or some pieces of eight—and come up with the money to buy it. The FOR SALE sign will be posted by morning, and you won't be quite so welcome once that goes up."

"I understand, sir," Booker said.

We thanked him for the ride and I pushed open the screen door of the market.

"Wow!" I said. "This smells so good."

Zee made a run for the open cases near the fish counter. "Look, Booker. Live lobsters. Tons of them."

Somehow I didn't think they'd be alive for long. Those crustaceans were a popular Vineyard dish.

On the opposite side was a glass-fronted refrigerator. LOBSTER ROLLS was written on a card taped to the door.

"Boy, do they look good," I said.

The lady working behind the counter called out to us. "They're on sale today," she said. "Two for the price of one."

Booker gave me a thumbs-up.

I reached in and pulled out the fattest rolls, the two that looked like they were stuffed with the most lobster meat. Then I opened the next compartment and got three bottles of water.

We were about to carry our lunch outside to eat on the dock, but when the door opened, I couldn't move.

A man and a kid my age came walking through it and stood face-to-face with us.

"Hey, Ezekiel," the kid said, forcing a smile as he looked at us. Then he said hello to Booker and me, too.

"Hey, Ross," Booker said. "Wassup?"

Ross Bagby, of course—one of the carousel bullies—and the older man must be his father.

Ross just shrugged his shoulders. I didn't know whether his passive manner was due to Zee's warning about the shark or the fact that his father was by his side. Either way, there was no sign of his rudeness today.

"Thanks, by the way," Ross said to Zee. "Turns out there were sharks near the Chatham beach yesterday, so the lifeguard got everyone out of the water."

He was looking down when he spoke. Then he picked his head up. "Your app is awesome."

Zee seemed pleased by the compliment.

But I couldn't even look at the Bagbys' faces. My eyes were glued to the front of their T-shirts. Both Ross and his dad had stains all over them—large splotches of fresh red blood that had dripped down the front of their clothes.

16

"New friends, Ross?" his dad said, reaching out his hand to shake ours. "I'm Cole Bagby."

"Good to meet you, sir," Booker said. "Yeah, we met yesterday."

"Islanders?"

"No, no, we live in Manhattan, too. We're visiting my grandmother in O.B."

"Well, you've got the best eats on the Vineyard right in your hands," Mr. Bagby said, holding the door open for us to leave. "Are you feeling okay, dear? Sorry, I didn't get your name. You look like you've seen a ghost."

"Devlin," I said. "Devlin Quick."

"Don't worry, Devlin," Mr. Bagby said. "We didn't wrestle with a bear, if it's our clothes you're staring at. Ross and I caught some fish this morning—some sea bass—and I got a little messed up getting them unhooked."

"Don't you believe in catching and releasing?" I asked.

I didn't mean to be disrespectful, but I sort of couldn't help myself. "Aren't you supposed to throw them back into the water and buy your dinner here at Larsen's?"

"You still have to get the hook out to let the fish go," Mr. Bagby said. "The blood will come out of our clothes in the wash. It always does."

Booker, Zee, and I walked out and sat down on one of the wooden boxes on the edge of the dock. I used a plastic knife to cut each of the lobster rolls in three pieces.

"See that?" Booker said. "That's Mr. Bagby's boat."

He pointed to a boat that was tied up alongside the dock, with its name painted on the rear.

REVENGE was written in bold black print, outlined in red. The words CHILMARK, MA, its home port, were below the name.

"You know what I was taking pictures of when the police officer pulled into the Thaw farm?" Booker asked me.

"I have no idea, but this lunch is amazing," I said.

"Bagby's boat," Booker said, pulling up the photos on his iPhone.

Zee was too busy chowing down his lobster roll to get into the conversation.

"What do you mean?" I asked.

"Look," he said, scrolling through the photographs.

"You're kidding," I said, wiping the mayonnaise off my face. "Mr. Bagby was cruising in the pond, right below the sheep barn? Really? What if he had trespassed on our trespassing?"

"Yeah, that would have been very interesting," Booker said. "The return of the *Revenge* to Menemsha Pond. That's quite a coincidence."

"You know better than that," I said. "Sam says there is no such thing as a coincidence in detective work. There's always a reason behind the curious linking of events."

"Like what, in this case?" Booker asked.

"Hold up," I said, putting my finger to my lips. "You should never rush my deductions. Here come the Bagbys."

"How did you three get up here to Chilmark?" Mr. Bagby asked as he walked up to our spot on the dock.

Booker answered him. "We took the bus."

"Well, Ross and I could give you a speedy ride back in our boat," he said. "It's a beautiful day for a trip on the ocean. If you've never done it before, it's quite a treat, and it gives you an entirely different way to see the island."

"No, thank you," I said. My mother had always taught

me not to accept rides from strangers—except for cops in uniform—and I'm sure she meant even rich strangers who had boats.

But at the very same moment, Booker spoke up. He was excited by the offer. "Is that one yours, right there?"

"Sure is," Mr. Bagby said. "We're going to eat our crab cakes on board and then head out to sea. Why not come along?"

"Why did you name her *Revenge*?" I asked, trying to make Booker get my point. "Was it after a pirate ship?"

"No. No, it isn't."

"You mean it's just a coincidence that Lemuel Kyd sailed in these very waters and had a ship named *Revenge*?" I said.

"I've never heard of Lemuel Kyd," he said.

"Really?" I said. He must have heard the sarcasm in my voice. "You're a Vineyard summer person, so you probably know a lot of the folklore. You're right here in Menemsha Pond, where Kyd hid from the Spanish and you never—"

"How about Blackbeard?" Mr. Bagby said, interrupting me. "He sailed all up and down the New England coast and he had a ship called *Revenge*."

Zee spoke up quickly. "Blackbeard's ship was named *Queen Anne's Revenge*," he said. "Different thing."

"Well, my vessel is named for the HMS *Revenge*," he said.

"HMS?" I asked.

"Her Majesty's Ship," Zee said, picking the biggest pieces of lobster claw out of his roll to chew on separately so his sandwich would last longer. "That's how the British fleet is named, all for Her Majesty or His Majesty."

"Exactly right," Mr. Bagby said. "Sir Francis Drake sailed the *Revenge* into battle in the Spanish Armada. That's why I chose it for my little boat."

I wasn't giving up without a fight.

"That word is kind of a mean name for a boat, don't you think?" I said. "Revenge is all about causing injury to someone—"

Mr. Bagby nodded his head in my direction. "It's about causing injury or insult to someone who injured you first."

"Who insulted *you* first, sir?" I asked.

"You do a very good cross-examination, Devlin," Bagby said. "I guess you're going to be a lawyer when you grow up."

"An investigative journalist," I said. "Just like my dad."

"Someday I'll tell you that story, young lady. It might

make a good article for you to write," Mr. Bagby said, taking his bag of crab cakes and walking to the steps that led down to the dock. "Let's go, Ross. We're on a schedule."

"Were you fishing at Tarpaulin Cove yesterday?" I asked him.

He stopped in his tracks and looked at Ross. "Must you tell people everything we do?"

"But, Dad, I didn't say a word about it," Ross Bagby whined to his father.

I tried not to snicker but it was tough.

"Or was the fishing better today inside the pond?" I asked. I didn't mean for Ross to get blamed for something that Artie Constant had told us.

Mr. Bagby's head snapped in my direction. "Ross just told me that you're a Ditchley girl, aren't you? Well, maybe the instructors there should spend more time teaching manners than on perfecting your skills at being busybodies."

Wilhelmina Ditchley had founded her school for girls almost a century ago. She prided herself on encouraging young women under her care to develop an inquisitive nature. I was happy to think that generations later, her wisdom had inspired me to question things at every turn. Our school motto, after all, is "We Learn,

We Lead." I find it impossible to learn unless I ask loads of questions.

"Ross didn't tell us anything about where you'd been. Booker and Zee and I—well, we try to be really observant."

Cole Bagby stepped onto his boat and Ross followed him by leaping off the dock. Neither one of them waved good-bye, which didn't surprise me.

We watched them start the motor and cruise till they got out of sight—till the letters that spelled *Revenge* looked smaller than the letters on the bottom row of the eye chart at my doctor's office.

The three of us walked down the road to the Texaco station and sat on the bench to wait for the bus.

I took out my phone and Googled Cole Bagby.

"It would have been fun to take that boat ride back to Oak Bluffs," Booker said.

"You don't even know those people," I said, waiting for the information to load. "Yesterday, you would have bopped Ross Bagby on the nose if you could have, and now it seems to me his father isn't entirely honest."

"I wanted to go with them, too," Zee said.

"All that blood kind of freaked me out," I said.

"You heard the man," Booker said. "Fish bleed, just like people do. It's as simple as that."

"'Does Cole Bagby have a bag of tricks'?"

"Why would you say that?" Booker was on his feet, watching a small yacht refill its gas tanks at the dock behind us.

I held up my phone. "I didn't say it. It's a headline in a magazine article about the man."

"Let me see," Booker said.

Booker was skimming the piece, scrolling as fast as he could. "Seems that Mr. Bagby owns a chain of restaurants."

"That's not the point," I said. "Keep reading."

"He's a numismatist," Booker said.

"Numismatists are coin collectors," Zee said. "Those guys love doubloons."

"How could you possibly know what that word means?" I said, giving Zee a playful nudge in the side.

"I figured everybody knows that. Numismatics is the study of coins," Zee said. "That's how come I bought all those reproduction pirate coins when Becca took me to the museum. To study them."

"Well, I sure didn't know," I said.

"You were kind of right not to accept a ride from the man, Dev," Booker said. "Bagby and his bag of tricks? The whole point of this article is that Cole Bagby tried to pass off some fake coins at a Numismatic Society event."

"Sometimes, like Sam says, you've just got to go with your gut instincts."

Zee jumped to his feet. "Were they fake pirate booty?"

Booker handed me back my phone. "Yup. Just phony old things with a portrait of Sir Francis Drake on them."

"I knew he was a crook," I said. "He had a slimy look to him."

"Just 'cause he had fish goop on his clothes? That's the stuff that looked really slimy," Booker said. "But I don't think it would hold up in court."

"I didn't get to the end of the article," I said. "Was Mr. Bagby arrested for passing fake coins?"

"Nope. Just kicked out of the society."

The bus turned the corner and came driving down the road toward the gas station.

"I, for one, am glad we didn't take a ride with the Bagbys," I said, standing up and digging in my pocket for the bus pass. "I wouldn't want him anywhere near our valuable doubloon."

17

"Tonight is all about tradition, Dev," Becca said. "It's my favorite night of the summer."

I like tradition as much as the next girl, but it just seemed crazy for me not to be able to solve the puzzle of who is the rightful owner of the doubloon before I had to leave the island on Saturday, and it was already Wednesday evening.

"Do you think Jenny Thaw will be at her house in the Campground tonight?" I asked. "It would be amazing if we could meet her."

"I heard from the butcher in town that Jenny went off-island last week," Becca said. "Hard to imagine anyone with a house in the center of all the action would ever miss Illumination Night, but we'll see."

"The butcher told you?" I asked. "There are no secrets in this town, are there?"

"Very few. And what there are," Becca said, "are always out of the box in a day or two."

She dimmed the lights in the kitchen and living room.

"Gentlemen," she called out to Booker and Zee, "are you ready to go?"

"We're on the porch, Becca," Booker said. "Couldn't be hungrier."

This tradition involved a lot of food, as Vineyard things usually did.

We headed off to Circuit Avenue for dinner at Fat Ronnie's. Apparently, Ronnie didn't consider the name an insult, since he chose it for himself. He served the biggest and best burger on Martha's Vineyard, and we weren't the only people who thought so.

"We're going to be late," Zee said, looking at the length of the line.

"I've had this timing under control for the last fifty years or so, so just hush up."

After we ate our burgers—piled high with cheese and pickles and lettuce and just about everything else you could get your mouth around—Becca led us to the side of the bakery halfway down the block where an operation called Back Door Donuts stayed open half the night serving fritters and donuts right out of the oven as they prepared the front counter of the bakery for the morning rush.

"I couldn't eat another thing," I said. "What's next?"

"We're off to the Tabernacle, where the Camp Meeting Association is," Becca said. "Back around the time of the Civil War, a whole lot of religious communities began to have meetings. Right here in Oak Bluffs is where John Wesley started the Methodist movement. People camped out in large tents for a week or two at a time, built up around a central tabernacle to join in a community of prayer and such."

"So we'll be sitting in tents?" I asked.

"Hardly," Becca said.

"They were all replaced ages ago by cottages," Booker said. "Dozens and dozens of tiny cottages painted all different colors, sitting as close together as it was possible to build them. Wait till you turn the corner and see it, Dev. It's like a gingerbread village."

I put out my arm to stop Becca. "Don't look now, but there goes Artie Constant," I said. "He's headed into the Campgrounds."

"Maybe he's two-timing me with another granny since I turned him down for a date tonight," Becca said. "I wouldn't blame him if he does."

"Keep an eye on him, Booker, will you?" I said.

"Just relax and have a good time tonight, Dev," he said.

"I plan to do that. I just never lose track of my surroundings, either."

But I almost did! When we squared the block and followed the growing crowd past the Wesley Hotel and into the narrow street behind the hotel, it was like stepping back into another century.

There were gingerbread cottages—like a village of oversize dollhouses—as far as I could see in every direction. They were trimmed in yellow and red and bright blue paint, and there was one that was entirely the color of pink bubble gum from roof to foundation.

"Grab some seats," Becca said, and Zee rushed ahead of us.

In the center of the large square, surrounded mostly by houses and one large church, was the Tabernacle—a large circular structure with a roof, but no sides, where people gathered for church meetings. Whatever religious purpose it usually served, tonight it was just a festive place to be.

Becca took the aisle seat so she could greet all her friends and neighbors. Zee sat beside her and then Booker and me.

The band came onto the stage and the bandleader tried to get everyone's attention to start the community sing.

Booker slumped down in his seat. "This is the nerdiest thing I've ever done."

"Ever?" I said, giggling at his comment. "I could name a few others."

"Every year I say I'll never do this again, and every year Becca takes my ear and twists it until I give in."

The first piece was "This Land Is Your Land," and the audience came to life singing along with the familiar music and words. Folk song after folk song followed. If Booker was waiting for a Bruno Mars or Demi Lovato hit to stir the crowd, I knew he was going to be disappointed.

"Check it out," he said. "On the other side of the aisle."

"The three bullies," I said, looking over. "Last guys I imagined at a sing-along."

The trio seemed to be with a woman, probably the mother of one of them. They didn't look too happy to be at the event. In fact, Emil leaned over and whispered something to the woman, then all three of them got up and marched out to the back, behind the last row of benches.

Must be something like a horse. You can drag a teenager to water—or in this case a sing-along—but you sure can't make him sing. Booker just crossed his arms and was probably wishing he was somewhere else right now, too. I found myself enjoying it, though.

Everyone stood for the finale—"God Bless America"—and then Becca leaned over to tell me to turn around facing the rows of houses.

The bandleader thanked everyone and announced that tonight's ceremonial honor of starting the first lights of Illumination Night would go to Mr. and Mrs. Bernard Carl. Everyone clapped, and in an instant, a white cottage trimmed in aqua went from appearing to be a dark shadow to a glowing beacon of light. The Carls must have been the people on the porch getting the illumination under way.

"What is all that?" I asked.

"Those are paper lanterns all over the porch and the deck and the rafters of the house. Each one is very delicate, and each has a small bulb inside," Becca said.

There must have been twenty of them illuminating the Carl Cottage, and within two minutes, every other house that formed part of the circle around the Tabernacle was bathed in the warm glow of lighted lanterns—hundreds and hundreds of them—outlined against the darkened little buildings and the navy blue night sky.

"That's the prettiest thing I've ever seen," I said to

Becca. I was twirling in a circle, taking in all the colors and all the decorations.

"You're right about that."

"Are you ready to go now?" Booker asked, yawning and stretching his arms. "The Game Room is open. We can hang out there."

Zee was yawning, too, but trying to fight it. "Can I go with them, Becca?"

The Game Room was an arcade, right on Circuit Avenue. Kids could go without parents, and it was where all the teenagers met to chill at the end of a summer day.

"You're coming home with me, Zee," she said. "And you two can stay out till ten-thirty That's almost another hour."

"You're forgetting something," I said, grabbing the back of Booker's shirt. "Aren't we going to say hello to Jenny Thaw?"

The lanterns were strung together like enormous orbs and hung from building to building, up and down the frames of the houses, and covering every porch.

"Look, Dev," Booker said, "a couple of girls from my school are going to be at the Game Room tonight. Why don't we just go there?"

"Are we into pirate treasure or not?" I asked, hands on my hips.

"All right. All right," he said. "Five minutes, okay?"

Becca had Zee's hand in hers, and he was leaning against her. "See the Carls' cottage? Count five to the right. That's where Jenny Thaw lives," she said. "If she's on the island, you can be sure she'll be out on the porch, meeting and greeting everyone."

Booker and I said good night to Zee and made our way around the back of the benches. The Carls were on their porch with the front door wide open. Mr. Carl was dressed in a tuxedo and top hat, and his wife had an old-fashioned dress on, with a huge bustle at the back and lots of lace at the collar.

"Come in and look around," the elegant woman said to us.

"Another time," I said. "Thanks so much."

The second, third, and fourth houses over were all lit up in the same fashion, and doors were ajar with Vine-yarders strolling in and out to see the unusual style of the funky old houses on this one-night-a-year opportunity.

When we reached the fifth house, there was a slim woman alone on the porch, rocking back and forth in a creaky chair. The bright blue and yellow lanterns above her head were strung across the beams like a long neck-lace of sparkling jewels.

"You're welcome to come in," she said, waving us up the steps, as two older women walked out the door from the house, thanking her for the visit.

I didn't have to ask if she was Jenny Thaw. She was dressed in an old-style gingham outfit and had scarlet silk ribbons in her braided hair. At the top of the steps, she was flying the Jolly Roger.

18

"How do you do, Ms. Thaw?" I said, reaching out my hand as Booker and I joined her on the porch.

"Lovely night, isn't it?" she said. "Have we met before?"

"No, no," Booker said. "We were at the sing with my grandmother, Rebecca Dylem, and she pointed out your cottage to us. Said we should give you her regards if you were at home."

"We have no choice but to be here on Illumination Night if our houses are along the front row, facing the Tabernacle," Jenny said. "Seven generations of Thaws have sat right where I am, welcoming all the gawkers."

"For some reason—maybe it was one of Becca's stories—I thought all the Thaws lived in Chilmark," I said.

"There was a time that most of them did," Jenny said.

She never stopped her rocking for a minute, even while she talked to us. I figured she was about forty years old, although it was hard to tell because of the costume and hairstyle. She kept one arm on the rocker to keep it moving, the other rested on top of a small wooden box on her side table, an antique tea caddy, like I had seen at my grandmother's home.

"That's a fun costume," I said. "Why are you dressed like that?"

"I do it to honor one of my ancestors," Jenny said. "My favorite of all the Thaws."

"That's a nice idea. Did you know her?"

Jenny smiled. She had an easy manner and was very pleasant to us. "Only in my imagination," she said. "She lived a very long time ago. In Chilmark, as a matter of fact."

"Do you mean Gertie Thaw?" I asked, bursting with enthusiasm, mostly because the subject had come up so naturally.

"So you've heard of her?" Jenny asked.

"Booker and I were on the beach yesterday when that shark swam by, and since she has the same name, we heard stories about Gertie all day," I said.

"And I could tell you more stories all night."

"Can you really?"

"Well, I'm exaggerating, but Gertie was the relative I most admired growing up," Jenny said. "Have a seat."

"We can't really stay," Booker said.

I hope this wasn't going to be our future, I thought to myself. Video arcade nonsense interfering with the chance to accomplish some real detecting.

"C'mon, Booker," I said. "Take a few minutes to listen."

He leaned his back against the upright post at the top of the steps.

"Are you dressed just like Gertie used to?" I asked.

"This dress was actually hers," Jenny said. "Gertie sewed her initials into the hem, all those years ago. It'd been in a chest up in the attic at our old farm till the place was sold a while back."

"And the Jolly Roger? That's because of Lemuel Kyd?" I asked.

"It sure is. Just a reproduction, of course, but I loved that girl's spunk, having a pirate for a boyfriend."

Booker put his sneaker on the tip of my shoe and pressed down. That was some kind of signal for me to cut to the chase.

"What about Kyd's treasure?" I asked.

"I'll add you two to the list of people out hunting for it, okay?" Jenny said, throwing her head back with the rocker and laughing again. "Folks have been doing that for years."

"Was the story true, though?" Booker asked. "Do you think Kyd gave any of his treasure to Gertie?"

"Here's what I know," Jenny said. "*Everybody* knows, really."

Booker and I exchanged glances, and I raised my eyebrows.

"After Lemuel Kyd left the island, Gertie spent a lot of years of her young life waiting for him to return, which never happened."

"Kind of sad, don't you think?"

"Once her ma and pa died, her brothers took over the property for themselves and their families," Jenny Thaw said. "Came to be that there was no room left on the farm for Gertie herself."

"But she could knit, couldn't she?" I asked. "She could sew clothing like the dress you're wearing tonight?"

"And so could the wives and daughters of all her brothers," Jenny said. "They had no use for the girl after the pirates left her high and dry."

"So there was no treasure at all," Booker said.

Jenny sat up straight and wagged her finger at him. "I never quite said that, did I?"

He waited a few seconds before he asked, "Well, what became of it?"

"Most of us in the family came to think that Gertie's big brother, Travis, took it from her."

"Stole it?" I asked.

I always hated being an only child, but if I had a brother who stole gold doubloons from me, that would be even worse than having no sibs at all.

"If she ever had it, yes," said Jenny. "Nobody knows whether Lemuel Kyd gave Gertie part of his treasure, or whether he buried it somewhere on the land, near the Pond."

"In which case," Booker said, "it might still be there."

"Oh, Lord," Jenny said. "Lots of men have broken lots of shovels looking for that booty."

At least Zee hadn't had time to break his plastic shovel this morning.

"But whether he forced the treasure out of her hand or dug it up from under her nose, Travis Thaw wound up being a very rich man with the biggest farm in Chilmark, and Gertie found herself living in this little old tent, before she was my age."

"It was really a tent once?" I asked.

"In 1836? Oh yes, this little house was really a tent back then," Jenny said, knocking on the wooden wall behind her. "Took another fifty years to make it look like this."

"So there were no rafters to hide things in," I said, looking as dejected as I sounded.

"No cubbyholes, no basement," she said. "That nasty

old brother left Gertie with nothing at all. Nothing but her pirate memories and some tattered silk ribbons."

"Well, maybe Travis became rich farming the land," Booker said.

"Not that kind of rich," Jenny said.

"I hope you don't think me rude, Ms. Thaw," I said, "but if he got that rich, why are you still living in this little cottage, with people so close on either side of you that when you sneeze they can probably hear you."

"That they can," she said.

She was smiling again, talking with her hands. She had no jewelry on—no bracelets or rings or earrings—and even though her dress was a costume, there was no attitude about her.

"You see," she told us, "I'm not a direct descendant of the Travis Thaw that was Gertie's brother. Do you understand what I mean?"

Both Booker and I nodded our heads.

"My great-great-great—well, I've lost track of how many greats we have to go back—but my direct ancestor was Zachary, the brother who was younger than Travis but older than Gertie."

"Did he, well, did he pass down any stories, Ms. Thaw?" I asked.

"He died young. He caught some kind of fever after

the birth of their child and was dead before he was twenty-three. His widow moved into this cottage after Gertie passed on."

"Sorry to hear that."

"I'm telling you," she said, "Travis elbowed everyone in the family out of anything Lemuel Kyd left for Gertie."

I didn't like stories with unhappy endings.

"Didn't Lemuel Kyd ever come back this way, looking for Gertie, or for his treasure?"

"Legend has it, young lady, that he was caught and hanged before he ever sailed these waters again."

I shook my head.

"Go on, you two," Jenny said as a couple came up the porch steps behind us. "Feel free to look around the house. It'll only take you a minute. There are times it feels like living in a beehive."

"Thanks," I said.

"Watch your head on the beams," she said. "You're both tall, aren't you?"

Booker led me in. The front room was a parlor with three chairs and two small round tables. "Tight quarters," he said.

The next room was a dining room with a table that

would seat six, and a small kitchen beyond that. I started up the narrow staircase.

"What's left to see?" Booker asked. "This place is creeping me out."

"We're here, aren't we? It's kind of cool to think we're walking exactly where Gertie Thaw walked, isn't it?"

"Like you said," Jenny Thaw called out, "I can hear it all. Go on up, kids. I've got a couple more of Gertie's dresses laid out on my bed, so you can see how she lived."

I took the rest of the steps in twos. The lamp next to the bed cast a dim glare, but the glow of all the lanterns hanging outside lighted the interior in a ghostly sort of way. There was a going-to-church kind of outfit lying across the pillow, and a work dress with a yellowed apron at the foot of the bed.

I turned around and scooted past Booker.

I picked up a bonnet that was on the dresser and playfully put it on. Booker shook his head and mouthed the word "loser" to me. I replaced it on the dresser.

But when I took my hand away, my fingers scraped over something that felt sticky—something that was on the surface of the dresser. Something that maybe Jenny hadn't had time to clean up before company began to arrive.

I didn't want to touch anything because it was too dark to see whether what I felt on my skin could stain any of the fabric of Gertie's antique clothing or Jenny's bedding.

"Booker," I whispered to get his attention. "I don't want to make a mess. Can you help me?"

"I'm out of here, Dev," Booker said, with one foot on the first step down.

"Don't bail on me," I said, but he was already on his way.

I crossed the narrow hallway to push open the door with my pinkie and peek in the bathroom, which was about the smallest one I'd ever seen.

I needed to turn on the faucet to wash my hands, so I flipped the light switch.

I jumped back when I looked down. The sticky stuff had left a red streak across the tops of my middle fingers, and the very same substance was dripping on the side of the sink.

"Booker," I said a little louder, but he was already down the stairs.

I had to tell myself to calm down. The goo was too bright to be blood, I was pretty sure. I hesitated before I turned on the faucet, but my curiosity got the better of me. That, my mother liked to remind me, was one of my biggest problems.

I sniffed the tip of my finger. The red stuff smelled familiar, but I was so frazzled at the moment I couldn't place it. It had a sort of chemical odor, the kind that made your nose twitch and your head pull away.

Then I saw a nail file—a disposable emery board—in the wastebasket next to the sink. I reached in and picked it up. Jenny must have used it for something because it looked a bit worn, but it was perfectly clean.

I ran the thin board from the top of the dripping line in the sink all the way down to the drain before blowing on the red stuff to make it dry.

I held open the pocket of my hooded sweatshirt— the new one that had INKWELL written across the back of it—and carefully put the nail file inside.

Then I rinsed my hands, drying them on the front of my jeans.

There was no telling what Booker would make of the red ooze I had recovered from Jenny Thaw's sink, but I knew I had the NYPD's crime lab as a backup solution if it figured in the mystery of who owned our underwater doubloon.

19

"I'm afraid I made a bit of a mess in your bathroom," I said to Ms. Thaw. "There was some red, well, stuff and I had to wash my hands in your sink."

She was surrounded by passersby enjoying Illumination Night. I had hoped she would tell me what the drip was, but she skipped right by that.

"I made the mess myself," she said. "Just marking the new lanterns with the year I bought them."

That sounded logical. But marking them with what, I wondered.

"I have so many questions I'd like to ask you, Ms. Thaw," I said.

"Not the time for it," she replied. "Come by in a day or two. Afternoons best. I love talking about Gertie."

An older woman with an oversized backpack standing on Jenny Thaw's porch turned around. The pack smacked into me and I lost my balance, jumping down the steps backward.

Booker had taken off ahead of me, waiting at the end

of the path that led back to Circuit Avenue. "What took you so long?"

"Something spilled just before we got there," I said, withdrawing the emery board from my pocket and holding it under his nose. "Smell this."

"Phew," he said. "That stinks. What is it?"

"I don't know, but Jenny said she was using it to date her new lanterns."

"Could be true. Like a marker or something."

"Markers aren't drippy."

"Ink is," Booker said.

"It doesn't smell like ink," I said, testing it again before I put it back in my pocket. "I'd really like to ask her about it when we go back to see her."

He glanced at the time on his phone. "Look, we've got twenty minutes before Becca wants us home. Could we go to the Game Room and have some fun with my friends?"

I was trying to keep up with him. "Wait a minute. You weren't having fun with me all week? When did that stop?"

"I'm done with trying to figure out anything else about Gertie Thaw, Dev," Booker said. "I'm not going back to talk to this lady. You can't solve this mystery on your own. You're going to need Sergeant Wright to help you. We can't just trespass and try to dig things up all over the place. Tomorrow I'm going to the beach and you can come along or not, okay?"

"Of course I want to go to the beach," I said. "Why can't we do both?"

Booker's phone buzzed with the sound of an incoming text.

"If that's from one of those new girls we're going to meet," I said, "I guess you'd better tell me her name."

His annoyance changed to concern as he read the text.

"It's from Becca," he said. "She wants us to come right home."

"Now?"

"Right now," Booker said, breaking into a jog.

Becca was standing on the front porch when we arrived, legs planted firmly on the floor with her arms folded and a tennis racket dangling from her right hand. She had a scowl on her face. All the lights inside were blazing as if she was having a party, but I knew it was getting pretty close to her bedtime.

"Are you okay, Grandma?" Booker said, running up to her as fast as he could. "Is Zee all right?"

She put her finger up to her lips. "Hush up, now. Zee's sound asleep."

"What's wrong?" I asked.

"I haven't locked a door in the house in all the years I've been coming to Martha's Vineyard," Becca said.

It was an odd thing about close-knit communities like this one. I hadn't met anyone on this island who locked his or her door, but as the sergeant told us, there was barely any crime.

Becca had paused to take a deep breath. I noticed her hands were trembling.

"Zee and I came back from the Tabernacle, and the minute I opened the door, I knew somebody had been inside here," she said.

"A burglar?" Booker asked.

"The only light I left on when the four of us went out was the one in the front hallway, but the living room and dining room were all lit up," Becca said, ignoring his question. "The pillows I'd plumped on the sofa were out of place, and some of the letters from the Scrabble board I'd been playing with Zee last night had been knocked onto the floor."

"You think someone's still inside?" Booker asked, about to make a dash in the door.

"No, no, son," she said. "I've been through the house from top to bottom, once Zee closed his eyes."

"Armed with a tennis racket? You were going to

attack the guy with that?" Booker asked, giving her a hug. "You should have texted us right away."

"I didn't want to spoil your evening," she said. "Time enough to deal with this tomorrow. I didn't get real mad until I looked around some more."

"I know what you're going to tell us, Becca," I said, taking her arm to walk her back inside. I had a good nose for trouble, Sam Cody liked to say. "Someone broke in and stole our gold doubloon."

20

"You got that half right, Devlin," Becca said. "Some one—or ones—sure did break in."

She turned off all the lights except for those in the kitchen, closed all the curtains, and for the first time in as long as she could remember, she locked the front and back doors of her home.

Becca had made herself a cup of tea, and we were sitting at the kitchen table.

"You mean it's not missing?" Booker asked.

"I don't think so," she said.

"How can that be?" I asked.

"I waited for you to come home before I looked," Becca said. "I wanted to be sure the shades were pulled down and the curtains drawn, and I didn't want to be alone except for an eight-year-old boy."

"Did you hide it?" Booker asked.

"I did."

Becca stood up and walked to the refrigerator. She

opened the freezer door, reached her arm in past some frozen food and the trays of ice cubes, and pulled out the familiar brown paper bag. It was getting a bit ragged. When she handed it to me, I opened it and looked in. The gold coin was gleaming under the kitchen light.

"Some of my old tricks still work," she said, smiling at us.

"The freezer?" I asked. "That's where you hid the doubloon?"

"I don't have a safe. I sometimes keep my best earrings back behind the frozen hamburger patties," she said. "Nobody's ever looked there yet."

"Good thinking," Booker said.

"There was altogether too much town chatter about your treasure for me to go off and leave it in the living room tonight," she said. "And now I think I'll sleep with it underneath my pillow. There isn't anybody on this island who would dare try to move me once I start snoring."

I was sharing the room with Becca. She was right about that, I'm sure.

"So they didn't get anything," Booker said.

"Now you're jumping to conclusions," she said.

"What?" I asked.

"Remember that Zee had been playing with those

coins I bought for him at the pirate museum on the Cape?" Becca said.

"Yes, ma'am," I said. "He even had them stacked up on the front porch where everyone could see them."

"I put away almost all of them before we left, but I couldn't find two of them when it was time for us to go out," Becca said. "While we were walking around town tonight, I asked him about them, and he told me that the two that looked like the doubloon were on the sofa, where he'd been sitting."

"So those two are missing?" I asked. "Zee must be heartbroken."

"He doesn't know the first thing about it, and you two are not going to tell him, do you understand me?" Becca said.

"Of course," Booker said, and we both nodded.

"I'm going to call Sergeant Wright first thing in the morning and tell her what happened," she said.

"Great!" I said. "Booker and I can help her figure out who broke in here."

"Chances of that, young lady, are slim to none," Becca said. "It's an old-fashioned expression but it's powerfully accurate for you two tonight."

"What do you mean, Becca? It's what we're good at."

She leaned forward and clasped her hand over Booker's.

"I called your mother after Zee went to sleep," she said, looking at him. "And Zee's dad after that. He's coming here by this time tomorrow to be with us."

Becca turned to me next. "Then I talked to Blaine," she said, referring to my mother.

I slumped back in my chair. No good could come of that conversation in these circumstances. A mother who happened to be the New York City Police Commissioner was a tough combination when her kid was away from home and suddenly living in a crime scene.

"Blaine went ahead and booked you both on the eight thirty flight for New York tomorrow morning."

Booker looked as bummed as I felt.

"That's not fair," he said. "My vacation is only half over. They have to let us stay."

"I haven't even finished my school experiment," I said, although homework was the last thing on my mind.

Nobody would ever pull Sherlock Holmes off an investigation in progress, that much was certain.

"This has nothing to do with your mothers, kids," Becca said. "There's just no way I can assure them, after what happened tonight, that I can keep you two safe."

21

I had the gold doubloon tucked safely in my small crossbody bag when Becca took Booker and me to the airport Thursday morning.

Zee was really unhappy to have us go home ahead of him. We told him that my swim team practice and Booker's tennis coach had decided we needed an early start before the end of summer, but he was staying on with his grandmother and his dad for another week. I hugged him and told him how much fun it had been to spend time with him, and that we'd let him know what we found out about the real doubloon.

Becca made up a story about hiding his collection of fake coins before we'd gone out last night so that she didn't have to tell him about the burglary. Sergeant Wright and one of the detectives would be going over the house for clues while the four of us had breakfast at the airport.

The flight attendant made a bit of a fuss over Booker

and me because we were the only two unattended minors on the plane. It was only forty minutes from takeoff to landing at JFK Airport, so we didn't need much attending.

"My mom just texted me," I said as we taxied in from the runway to the gate. "Sam is going to meet us at baggage claim. She's in a meeting at the mayor's office about funding for the department."

"Lucky break," Booker said. "Imagine the questions she'd have for us."

"Don't remind me. I'll probably be grounded for illegal use of vacation time or some other made-up crime," I said.

We waited until most of the passengers had deplaned and then got off, making our way through the crowded terminal down the escalator to claim area six.

I could see the top of Sam's head above the crush of people pushing to reach for their luggage.

I lifted my arm above the cowboy hat on the man in front of me and waved. Sam saw my long arm and waved back. I ducked between the cowboy and his kid and went running to Sam, who wrapped me in a bear hug and lifted me four or five inches off the ground.

"I've missed you, Devlin," Sam said. "It's been way too quiet here without you, and your mother gets in kind of a grouchy mood when you're gone so long."

"I wasn't gone half as long as I was supposed to be," I said. "Plus, she's got Natasha—and Asta, too—to keep her company."

My mother had adopted a young woman from Eastern Europe who was now a graduate student at Columbia. Natasha had been orphaned as a teenager, and brought to America by very bad guys to do forced labor for them. My mother had been the prosecutor on the case, and when it ended, her bond with Natasha was so close that she offered to adopt her. I had grown up an only child, and now had a big almost-sister whom I idolized.

"Hey, Booker," Sam said. "That beach bum life too boring for you? Miss the action of the city?"

"Trust me. I could have stayed on the Vineyard another month," Booker said, pulling his bag off the conveyor belt while Sam reached for mine.

"Is she mad at us, Sam," I asked, as we headed with our wheeler bags to the unmarked SUV that was parked with a special NYPD identification plate right in front of the terminal.

"Us?" Booker said. "None of it was my idea, not from the first bucket of water you dipped—"

"She's not mad at all. She's as interested as you are to find out who the burglar is," Sam said, turning to

Booker with a smile. "And the cardinal role of being a partner to another crime fighter is to always have his back. Her back. Don't ever give her up, understand? None of this 'she wanted to do it but I really didn't.' Real partners don't do that."

Booker nodded.

We got to the car and Sam unlocked it. Booker got into the front seat and I climbed into the back.

Sam started the engine and picked up his cell phone, speed-dialing a number. "Tapp? It's Cody."

Andy Tapply was the sergeant who was assigned to the commissioner's office. He was at the desk immediately outside my mother's door. Loyal and kind and smart, he knew where she was every second of the day.

"Tell the commissioner it's ten fifteen and I'm pulling out of JFK. We're rolling," Sam said. "I've got Kid Blue."

Booker looked at me and grinned for the first time this morning. "I gotta say, the coolest thing about you is that the NYPD gives you your own nickname."

POTUS is how the media refers to the president of the United States, using each first letter of his title, and FLOTUS is always the First Lady. Since my mother was the first woman to be the NYPD's commissioner, leading the more than thirty thousand men and women in

blue uniforms, the chief of detectives gave her the nickname Lady Blue.

So when the cops were talking about me on the
phone or in texts or in communications when they
didn't want to use my name, they had taken to calling
me Kid Blue. I liked it—how special it felt—more than
I would ever admit.

"Now that you've got me," I asked, "what are you
going to do with me?"

"We're going to drop Booker off at home on the Upper
West Side," Sam said, "and then you're going straight to
the Puzzle Palace."

The address of NYPD headquarters was One Police
Plaza, or One PP. Detectives had given that building a
nickname, too: the Puzzle Palace. It kind of suited the
place, since there was so much mystery and intrigue
going on there.

The road out of the airport was a tangle of intersec-
tions and exits.

"So I know that JFK is in Queens, but I don't know
what this neighborhood is called," I said.

I knew Manhattan like the back of my hand, but I
was pretty weak on what New Yorkers called the Outer
Boroughs, like Queens.

"Jamaica," Sam said. "Jamaica, Queens."

Now the signs were pointing to the highway entrances ahead, offering several choices.

"How about the NYPD Crime Lab, Sam," I said. "Isn't that in Jamaica, too?"

"What's up your sleeve?" he asked. "I'm guessing this isn't a geography lesson."

"It was just a natural chain of thought," I said.

"Natural, because you've been out here to the Crime Lab?" Sam asked.

"Just the opposite. My mother wouldn't let me come because she thought it was too far for me to go on the subway alone. You need to transfer trains and all that stuff, but you could take us right there. Get Booker and me in the door."

"I just Googled it," Booker said. "NYPD Crime Lab. It's on Queens Boulevard in Jamaica. The last sign I saw said that's just two exits away."

It was obvious to me that the burglary of his grandmother's home had put his head right back in the mystery of our gold doubloon.

"I take my orders from the police commissioner," Sam said, "in case you didn't remember that. And she wants you at One P.P."

"Here's the thing, Sam," I said. "Booker and I found this coin."

"I know all about your caper," Sam said. "A gold doubloon. Now, word is out all over and you two are such a hot property that the commissioner had to airlift you out of the Vineyard."

"Yeah, it seems like town criers are a dime a dozen on that island," I said, shaking my head. "And I've got the coin right here, in my bag, around my neck."

"Your secret is safe with me," Sam said, never taking his eyes off the road. "I promised your mom I'd fight off any pirates that came too close to us before I could put you safely in her care."

"C'mon Sam, sooner or later my mother is going to have to send a team of detectives right out here to Jamaica to have the coin examined," I said, "when we can make a simple detour and be on our way home in an hour."

"Examined for what?" he asked.

"There's something on the coin, some kind of spot or stain," I said, leaning forward against the back of Booker's seat. "Booker and I have no idea what it is, but I bet someone at the lab can tell us. We've done everything by the book—handled the coin with gloves, kept it in a paper bag—"

"What does the stain look like?" Sam asked.

"It's red. That's all we can tell you about it."

"Red—like blood?" he asked.

"It's probably not blood," I said.

"Maybe we're making something out of nothing," Booker said, "but a bunch of weird stuff has been going on since we found this coin. I was ready to give up on all this, but now there's been a burglary and a theft—real crimes, Sam."

I nodded in agreement.

"What would be the harm if someone at the police lab could just tell us what's on the coin?" Booker asked. "Dev's right. You know Aunt Blaine will make someone come back out here and analyze it later on."

"Haven't I got enough of a battle on my hands just going one-on-one with Devlin?" Sam asked Booker.

"Aren't you the guy who just told me I always had to cover my partner's back?" Booker said. "I'm one hundred percent behind Dev on this one."

The large green highway sign had a white arrow pointing to the exit lane. QUEENS BOULEVARD—JAMAICA.

Sam Cody put his blinker on, moved into the right lane without a second to spare, and swerved off the highway onto the service road.

"I can't argue with that," he said to Booker. "Let's put these lab techs to the test."

22

"Let's just assume that the lady whose face is on this coin is Queen Isabella of Spain," I said to Officer Hadley.

"Okay," he said.

Greg Hadley was a young cop who'd been assigned to the Crime Lab right out of the Police Academy, he told us, because of his college double major in biology and chemistry. Booker and I were sitting on either side of him in his cubicle at the lab, while Sam had coffee with some of the older detectives he knew.

"Facts," I said, as Hadley gave us vinyl gloves to put on. "We found this coin in the water—"

"Fresh or salt?"

"Salt," I said. "It was sort of on the top of a layer of sand, about ten feet off the beach. Booker's cousin scooped it up in a plastic pail, and we haven't let anyone touch it since."

"Do you have any idea how long it was in the water?" Hadley asked.

"Nope," I said.

"We were hoping you'd tell us it had been there for a couple of hundred years," Booker said.

Hadley laughed, holding the coin by the edges and turning it around under the light on his worktable. "Sorry to disappoint you. I can't tell whether it was submerged a week ago or two centuries."

"The gold looks so shiny," I said.

"Salt water can be very corrosive," Hadley said. "It can make a mess of coins that are made of silver or copper, but it really doesn't hurt gold at all."

"So we still don't know how long our doubloon was underwater," I said.

"That's right."

"Next to Isabella's ear," I said, "there's some red stuff."

"I see it," Hadley said. He put the coin under a scope of some kind that must have magnified it. "That hasn't been in the water for very long, and it didn't make the trip over here from Spain two hundred years ago, either."

"You know what it is?" Booker asked.

"Not yet," Hadley said. "This is a science lab, not a workbench with a crystal ball."

"You want more facts?" I asked.

"What have you got?" Hadley said, as he studied the spot under his scope, touching it with a tiny metal tool that looked thinner than a toothpick.

I took a deep breath. "There are two different things we're trying to figure out," I said.

"Wait a minute," Hadley said, looking up from his scope. "Cody said this was a school experiment of some kind."

"That's how it all started," I said. "I was looking for fish scale DNA, not trying to find buried treasure. But then we came up with this doubloon, and Booker and Zee and I would like to return it to its rightful owner. We think it may have been stolen."

"Fair enough," Hadley said.

"But the police on Martha's Vineyard didn't have any reports of stolen property," Booker said. "So we were trying to identify who its owner might be."

"Or whether it's a finders-keepers kind of thing," I said, "because it's so old and was just lost ages ago in the sand and water."

"But then last night someone broke into my grandmother's house and tried to steal it," Booker said.

"This sounds really serious," Hadley said. "Do the Vineyard police have any suspects?"

"They hadn't even started their investigation when

we left the house this morning," I said, "but Booker and I have a few."

Greg Hadley put down the coin, pushed back his chair, and looked from Booker's face to mine.

"Shoot."

I took another deep breath. My mother had taught me that you really had to be careful before you point fingers at people.

"Not exactly suspects," I said, speaking slowly, "but persons of interest."

Hadley folded his arms. "You sure are your mother's daughter. So who are you two interested in?" he asked.

"Well, first of all, there's this old guy who's keeper of the lighthouse in Oak Bluffs," Booker said. "His name is Artie Constant. He's kind of an expert on all things related to pirates, and he was really anxious to see our doubloon."

"He knew about it?" Hadley asked.

Booker hung his head. "By the end of the day, it seemed like everyone knew about it. But we're to blame for telling Artie."

"Now here's a fact about Artie," I said, backing up Booker's point. "He's restoring the outside of the lighthouse, and he had a barrel full of red paint right at the foot of the staircase."

"You saw the paint?" Hadley asked.

"I fell into it," I said. "I was pretty clumsy coming down that huge staircase."

Hadley laughed. "Did it stain your clothes?"

"Booker's grandmother washed my T-shirt. The paint came right out," I said, "and it washed off my skin easily, too."

"I can test this for paint, but I doubt that's what it is," Hadley said. "Paint wouldn't make it underwater for even twenty-four hours without chipping some. Especially with sand around it and a current making waves on the beach. That would scratch the surface, and I just don't see any marks in this spot."

"Even if it's not Artie Constant's red paint," Booker said, "that doesn't mean he's not the guy who broke into my grandmother's house, looking for gold."

"Of course not," I said. "After all, he was really pushing to take Becca out for the evening, wasn't he?"

"Don't get ahead of yourselves, kids," Hadley said. "You got another character?"

"The next ones are actually a trio," I said. "A trio of bullies."

"I've got no use for bullies," Hadley said.

Booker told Hadley the story of Zee and the carousel, and how we ran into Ross Bagby and his dad at Larsen's Fish Market the next day.

"You say the kid's dad is a coin collector?" Hadley asked.

"I found an article about him online," I said. "I'm going to ask Sergeant Tapply to run a background check on him for us."

"You've got the best connections in the Puzzle Palace," Hadley said. "I better stay on my toes here."

"So when we ran into Ross and his dad," Booker said, "they were covered in blood from head to toe."

"Blood? Are you sure?"

"Fish blood," Booker said. "They'd caught some sea bass on their way to sneak around this old farmhouse."

No point in my correcting Booker. We were the ones sneaking around the farmhouse. The Bagbys were sneaking around on the pond.

"Okay," Hadley said. "That's easy. I just need a pinprick of the spot to test it for blood, but I'm pretty sure it's not that either. The color is too bright."

"Too bright?"

"It's oxygen that makes blood bright red," Hadley

said. "When blood dries outside the body—yours or Moby Dick's—it dries much darker."

"Well, the three of them are still bad dudes," I said. "They were incredibly mean to Booker's cousin."

"Guilty of that," Hadley said. "Anyone else?"

"Last night we met this woman named Jenny Thaw who comes from the family that may actually have a claim to the gold," I said. "We were invited into her home."

"So what was in this lady's place?" Hadley asked. He seemed eager to get back to his own cases, with folders stacked on his workbench. "Blood? Paint? Tomato juice?"

I cleared my throat. "Glop."

"What?"

"I don't know what," I said. "It was some kind of gloppy red stuff that had spilled on her table and in her bathroom sink."

"I never solved a crime with glop," Hadley said, "but there's always a first. Can you be more specific?"

I opened my crossbody bag again and removed the emery board.

Hadley looked at it, took it from me in his gloved hand, and then nodded at me.

"I mean, I didn't preserve it properly," I said, "but the chain of custody is good."

He turned it over in his hand. "Ms. Thaw gave you this?"

"Not exactly," I said. "The emery board had been thrown out in a wastebasket, so I think that was abandoned property."

"That's a legal search and seizure, Officer Hadley," Booker said. "Aren't we right?"

"I think any judge would go along with that," Hadley said, holding the emery board up to his nose. "Garbage is fair play."

"I just ran the board down the sink bowl and scooped up the red stuff," I said. "But I don't know what it is."

Hadley sniffed at the emery board again. "Did it smell when it was wet?"

"Yup. I know I've smelled it before, I just don't know where."

He pulled his chair back into the workbench and examined the spot on the coin under his scope again. Then he moved the coin aside and put part of the emery board in its place.

"I'm just going to take another pinprick from the coin," he said, "and a snip from your nail file. Is that okay with you?"

"You're in charge," I said.

"Seems to me that you're pretty much in charge, best as I can tell," Hadley said.

"Dev usually is," Booker said.

"Something about your maternal DNA?" Hadley asked.

"Must be," I said, shrugging my shoulders.

Hadley put both pieces of shiny red material on a single glass plate about two inches long and moved that under the scope.

"I'm comfortable telling you that until I do the chemical analysis on this," Hadley said, "it appears that the substance on the coin and the dried glop you captured on the emery board are the same."

"*Really?* That's kind of amazing," I said. "Are you going to find out what it is?"

"That's my plan," Hadley said. "But I've got some other work to do first."

"Booker and I can wait. That's okay."

Hadley shook his head. "I'll run some tests and call you later," he said, handing me back the gold coin. "And don't go jumping to any conclusions. I certainly can't tell you that the lady who had this stuff in her house is the person who put it on the coin. That could have happened months apart."

Hadley lifted the emery board to his nose again before he passed that back to me.

"There's something you're not telling us," I said. "What is it you smell?"

"This is what we call an educated guess," Hadley said. "You can't hold me to it."

"I promise." I couldn't stop wiggling, crossing my fingers and holding them tight.

"I spent a lot of time in chemistry lab, mixing compounds and agents—that's the educated part of it," Hadley said, "and the guess is just being around girlfriends."

"What's your guess?"

"I'm thinking this bright red spot is actually nail polish," he said, "the same thing that was dripping in Ms. Thaw's sink."

"Nail polish!" I exclaimed. I sniffed at the emery board. "Of course that's the smell. My mom gets a manicure every week, and sometimes when I go along with her the fumes are enough to make you sick."

"Every brand of nail polish has a different chemical formula," Hadley said. "I don't want to fill you up with fancy scientific terms right now, but there are ingredients to make the film less brittle, there are dyes to create the specific colors—like this bright red—and there are solutions to make it more difficult for water or oil to penetrate the polish after it's applied."

My mind was racing faster than Officer Hadley could fill it with an explanation of the polish ingredients.

"One thing is for sure," Booker said. "Jenny Thaw had nail polish in her house just last night."

"Right," I said. "She told me she was using whatever it was—I didn't know it was polish at the time—to mark the date of Illumination Night on her new lanterns."

"We can call her up and ask her about it," Booker said. "We can ask her if she knows about the doubloon, and if she had anything to do with the drop of red nail polish that's on the face of it."

"Now don't go calling anyone based on a mere hunch of mine," Hadley said, giving us his sternest expression. "I'll have a more reliable answer for you in a couple of days."

"But if we just ask her," I said.

"There are no 'buts' in a science laboratory," Officer Hadley said, standing up between us. "Especially one that's run by a police department. When I have an answer, based on results I can validate, then you can make all the calls you want."

"When will that be?" I asked.

"Today's Thursday," he said. "Monday at the very latest."

"Monday?" I asked. "You can't imagine all the terrible things that could happen between now and then."

I couldn't quite imagine them myself, but I didn't think Hadley would ask me to give him an example, and I was just trying to establish the urgency of all this.

"Hey, Cody," Hadley called out to Sam. "Ready for your next stop. You ought to take these two to be fitted for police officer uniforms. They'll be putting us out of a job, the way they're going."

23

"I'm okay, Mom," I said, squeezing her so tightly she could barely get out of the SUV and onto the sidewalk. Our detour to the crime lab made it smarter to drop me off at home, instead of One PP. "I really am."

Sam had dropped Booker and me at our homes and then gone downtown to wait for my mother to leave the office at five p.m. My dog, Asta—a totally lovable rescue—was so excited to see me that he could barely stop licking my cheek long enough to breathe.

"Sometimes I think being New York City's Police Commissioner is the easiest part of my life, Dev," she said, holding me at arm's length and spinning me around as though she was making sure all my parts were intact.

"It's not like Booker and I started out to cause any trouble," I said. "Stuff just happens to me."

I threw my arms around her again while Sam grabbed her briefcase and tote so she could return the big squeeze. I may be twelve, but my mother's affection and her approval still meant pretty much everything to me.

She held me close and kissed the crown of my head. I guessed there might be tears involved.

"Let's go upstairs so you can tell me all about it," she said. "Sam, will you stay for dinner?"

"Another time," he said, passing Mom's briefcase to me.

My mother had one arm around my shoulders, shepherding me toward the door of the building. She didn't let go of me for the entire ride up in the elevator.

Natasha had made a super-size serving of mac and cheese in honor of my return home—they even let me skip the salad—and I filled them in on everything that Booker and Zee and I had done. I showed them the gold doubloon and then Jenny Thaw's emery board, before Natasha left to meet up with her friends.

"Why do I get the feeling that you're leaving out some of the details of your adventures?" my mother asked as I cleared the table.

"I'm not hiding anything, Mom," I said. "It's just that everything was happening so fast it's hard to keep track of it all."

Every now and then I did have this habit of filtering out some of the things I had done, just so she wouldn't worry about my every move. After all, I didn't have a bodyguard like Sam to keep me out of harm's way.

"Want some ice cream?" she asked.

"Nope. It can't be as good as Mad Martha's."

My mother laughed. "So you're going full Vineyard on me, are you?"

"You did sort of cut my time up there short, didn't you? Booker and I were having a blast."

"I admire your search for the real owner of the old coin," my mother said, "and for the circumstances of its disappearance. But once there was a burglary at Becca's last night, I really had no choice but to bring you home."

I followed her into the living room. She sat on the far end of the large sofa and I curled up on the opposite side of it. She had the clicker in her hand and was about to turn on the TV to catch the local news.

"Are you ever going to take that bag off from around your neck?" my mother asked. "In a few days, you won't be able to hold your head up straight."

"I feel like it's the safest place for the coin at the moment."

"Have it your way," she said.

"Do you think the Oak Bluffs police sergeant is right?" I asked. "That the coin belongs to Booker and Zee and me because we pulled it up out of the water? Finders keepers and all that?"

"If Becca is right and enough people on the Vineyard

know about the coin, maybe the owner will come forward to claim it."

"Would someone have the right to claim it?"

"You want a mother's answer," she asked, "or a lawyer's answer?"

I smiled at her and stretched out my leg to poke her with my toes. "I love it when you can out-prosecute everybody else. Tell me."

"The law of the seas is a very complicated matter, Ms. Quick," my mother said. "Cases like this come before the highest court all the time."

She was talking like a judge now, using a British accent, too, to make me laugh.

"The main difference, the key question in these cases, is whether the discovery of the gold," she said, pausing to point at my crossbody bag, "is that the gold you're hiding was the result of treasure-hunting . . . or salvage."

"Salvage?" I asked. "What's that?"

"Salvage occurs when someone saves property that's adrift at sea, or abandoned. Under international law, the 'salvor' is required to return the goods to the original owner, in exchange for a reward."

"Well, we weren't treasure hunting," I said, "and it wasn't exactly a salvage operation—and I wouldn't begin to know who to return it to, since it wasn't part of a shipwreck so far as we can tell. And there should be some consideration for the fact that I was experimenting in the name of science."

"An excellent point for the defense," my mother said.

"When did I become the defense?" I asked, getting into her game. "I haven't done anything wrong."

"Then, are you likening yourself to Sir Isaac Newton, Ms. Quick?" my mother said. "He discovered gravity while sitting beneath someone's apple tree, so you believe that he was entitled to eat the apple? Is that it? I mean, identifying fish scales might entitle you to keep the fish that washed up on the Inkwell Beach, but I'm not so sure about the gold doubloon."

"Be serious, Mom. There's a lot at stake here," I said, changing positions to argue my case more effectively, drawing my knees up beneath me.

"You're right," she said. "I was just being silly. There's a rule in American law that refers to territorial waters, and from what you've told me about where the coin was, it's probably the property of Massachusetts."

She reached for the antique brass ruler on the coffee table in front of us. She lifted it and brought it down with a bang, like a judge's gavel on the bench.

"So ordered," she said.

I sat back on my heels and groaned.

"Don't be so glum, my dear," my mother said. "If no one comes forward to claim the pirate treasure, perhaps the state will give the coin to you after all."

"The state is a big place, Mom. How will the governor even know how to find me?"

"Just wear that ridiculous bag around your neck for another five or six years and everyone will know how to find you *and* that valuable coin."

"Mom! Be serious."

"I'm going in to take a refreshing bubble bath," she said, coming back to tousle my hair and kiss me on top of my head. "Think about doing the same, and getting a good night's sleep."

"Do you have any ideas to help us, Mom?" I asked. "Anything Booker and I should do?"

"The Oak Bluffs police have to handle the burglary, Dev, because it's a crime in their jurisdiction," she said. "They didn't come away with any leads this morning, but Sergeant Wright and I are going to talk to each other tomorrow. Okay?"

"Then you'll tell Booker and me what you find out, right? So we can work on this end of things and keep our piece of the investigation going."

"We'll see," my mother said.

"We'll see? Oh, Mom, that's just parent-code for 'no.' That's all those two words ever mean."

My mother laughed. "Hey, it took you twelve years to break the code."

"Just say yes. Please?"

"Okay, darling. Yes," my mother said. "Let's start fresh in the morning. You give me every fact, and I'll find out what Sergeant Wright knows and we'll put the whole picture together. Yes, you and Booker deserve to be part of all this."

I stood up on the sofa and jumped off, over the arm. "You're the best, Mom. Okay if I call Booker to tell him?"

"Of course it is," she said, removing her earrings and pearl necklace and kicking off her heels as she walked toward her bedroom.

"Great," I said. "We've got some ideas about what the cops need to do next. Or maybe Booker and I can take some of the basic assignments for ourselves."

It sounded like my mother was laughing as she walked off. "We'll see about that idea," she called out to me. "We'll just have to see."

24

"How did it get to be eight thirty?" I asked Natasha the next morning.

I was still in my pajamas. I walked into the kitchen, rubbing my eyes, and sat down at the table where she was reading the newspaper and sipping her coffee.

"Detective work is exhausting," Natasha said. "You must have worn yourself out on the Vineyard."

"Mom was supposed to wake me up before she left," I said, pouring myself a glass of orange juice. "We made a plan."

"Maybe it's something I can help with," she said. "I don't have class until one o'clock today."

Natasha was a journalism student in graduate school at Columbia University. She was a huge help with my homework—not to mention being there for me whenever I had problems to solve.

"Thanks anyway," I said, taking an English muffin from the refrigerator and popping it in the toaster.

"Booker and I are going to sit down with her to talk about what we can do in the doubloon investigation. We can take the train down to the Puzzle Palace and do it with her there."

Natasha put down the paper. "Sam came to pick Blaine up at five this morning," she said. She had been a teenager when she met my mother in the courthouse, and still called her by her first name. "There's a hostage situation on Staten Island. She won't be able to do that with you today."

"What kind of hostage situation?" I asked.

Getting the news that my mother was in the middle of a real-life police crisis was always frightening. I was as wide awake now as if someone had put a bunch of ice cubes down the back of my pajamas.

"Don't worry, Dev," Natasha said, placing her hand over mine. "She's just gone to the scene for moral support of her cops. She's not in danger."

"But what is it?"

"Some guy went into an all-night parking garage and had a fight with the workers, so he's keeping them locked up inside," Natasha said. "That means they are his hostages."

One minute my mother could be joking around with me and holding me close to her, and the next she was doing the most serious work in the city. She was Lady Blue to the entire police department, and the most important person in the world to me.

"Is Sam texting you?" I asked.

"Yeah. Every fifteen minutes."

"I'll get dressed and call Booker," I said. "Would you ask Sam to text me, too?"

"Sure," Natasha said. "Are you going somewhere?"

"Maybe we'll go to Headquarters to wait for Mom," I said.

"You can hang out with me, Dev," Natasha said. "She'll be safe, I promise you."

"Thanks," I said, finishing my juice and going inside to get dressed. "I'd sort of like to be where I can see Mom when she gets back to work."

"I get it," she said.

I called Booker and told him what was going on, and we met at ten fifteen to take the subway downtown.

Before we'd even gone one stop, Sam texted good news.

"Situation over! Everybody safe."

The photograph he sent showed my mother in the middle of the NYPD's hostage negotiators—the men and women who worked to get the victims released.

Like the rest of the team, she had an NYPD jacket over her light gray suit. On the back were the words TALK TO ME, the motto of the squad.

I smiled and texted back. "Always good advice. Tell her how proud of her I am."

I wanted to tell Sam to give her a big kiss for me, but I knew he wouldn't cross the line and do that.

"Lady Blue going to hospital to greet victims being treated for minor bruises. Then to press conference with the mayor. You and Booker should play tennis or chill. Later."

I was tempted to write back a message for my mother: "We'll see."

But I didn't need to make her day any worse, even if it was just a joke. So instead I texted: "Later," with a whole bunch of smiley faces.

"Change in plans," I said to Booker.

"For a good reason," he said. "You want to turn around and go home? We can pick up our rackets and go to the park to play tennis."

"I think we just got very lucky," I said. "Too lucky for me to let you trounce me in a game of tennis."

Booker played for the Hunter High team. He was too good for my game.

"There's one more lead the two of us can track down,"

I said. "If my mom and Sergeant Wright don't get this all together until Monday, which is the way it looks now, we may have some more evidence to help them. We'll get off at Twenty-Eighth Street," I said.

"Twenty-Eighth? What's there?"

"This whole thing started as an experiment about DNA," I said.

"Yeah. I know that."

"The NYPD does all its DNA work at the city's lab on Twenty-Sixth Street," I said. "Not the kind of stuff Officer Hadley did yesterday, in Queens. It's only DNA at this place."

"How can we get in without your mother?" Booker asked.

"I've been there with her a dozen times," I said, "and my mom invited three of the biologists to come to Ditchley to lecture to us for our STEM program. Getting in will be a piece of cake."

"Is this where your buckets of sand and fish scales are being analyzed?" Booker asked.

"No way," I said. "They'll be sent over to Cape Cod, to the institute that does work with ocean creatures. Our science teacher got the school to give us each an allowance to get lab results tested and sent to school."

I stood up and held on to the railing over my head, anxious to get off the train when it stopped at Twenty-Eighth Street.

"So DNA on what, Dev?" Booker asked.

"Start with the emery board," I said. "It's a nail file. It's bound to have DNA on it from being rubbed against someone's skin or nails."

"Jenny Thaw," Booker said. "What good is that?"

"At least we'd have her DNA profile," I said. "What if she's the one who broke into Becca's house? What if she has something to do with the coin, if it ever belonged to her relative Gertie?"

Booker stammered. "I—uh—I just never thought of anything like that."

"Then there's the coin," I said.

"C'mon, Dev. Don't be silly," he said. The train doors opened and I scooted out onto the platform, with Booker at my heels. "The coin was submerged in water for days, maybe months or years."

I stopped in my tracks and turned to face Booker, my hands planted on my hips.

"Did you see what Officer Hadley did yesterday?"

"Of course I did," Booker said. "I was standing right next to you."

"He pricked the red spot with some little metal tool to analyze it for us."

"Right," Booker said.

"And he explained that the ingredients in nail polish form a film or a coating, which keeps water from getting through or into the polish."

"I·heard that, too."

"So if we get someone at the DNA lab to scrape off some of the red stuff, even though the coin was in the water," I said, "there's a good chance that there could be a trace of human DNA on the surface of the coin, covered over by the polish."

"Whoa!" Booker said. "That would be amazing."

"Imagine if that DNA profile could prove to the police who owned the coin," I said, "or maybe the person who stole it. Someone who had a legal right to it would have claimed it by now. They wouldn't be breaking into houses to try to get it back."

"This experiment has turned you around," Booker said. "You were always all about books and literature and writing short stories. You were happy to live in the school library."

"I still am happiest in a library," I said, "but science is so interesting and so much fun."

"Now you're shooting to be the Marie Curie of the

Ditchley School," Booker said, running up the steps to the street ahead of me. "Two Nobel Prizes in Science."

"I'm not looking for any prizes," I said, trying to think the way Sam Cody would. "I just want to break this case."

25

"Devlin Quick," I said, presenting my school ID card to the security guard.

"Booker Dibble," he said. "Hunter High School."

The sign over the guard's head said OFFICE OF FORENSIC BIOLOGY.

I learned from my mom, back when I was just a young kid, that the word "forensics" meant the use of science in the law—especially in regard to evidence in criminal cases. This building was the brand-new city laboratory where all the DNA from police investigations was analyzed.

"Who are you here to see?" the guard asked.

"Kerry O'Donnell," I said.

"She's expecting you?" the guard asked.

"Not exactly," I said, trying to think of some excuse for being there.

The guard looked at my ID again. "You related to our commissioner?"

"I am," I said. "I'm her daughter."

"Should have said so to begin with," he said, writing our names in his logbook and directing us to the elevator. "O'Donnell's on six."

"Smooth as silk," Booker said.

The sixth floor labs looked like some kind of futuristic movie set. All the biologists were dressed in white lab coats. The workbenches had protective hoods covering them—if one scientist sneezed at her desk, without the hood it could contaminate the sample on the desk next door—and the workers each wore clear plastic goggles and white gloves.

Kerry's office was down the hall past the first bank of workbenches. When I got to the door with her nameplate on it, I knocked.

"C'mon in," she said.

"Excuse me," I said, opening the door.

"Dev! What a treat," she said, getting to her feet to greet us.

She was one of the youngest forensic biologists on the staff—super-smart, with a great sense of humor. Even when she came to school and talked about the most complicated science issues, Kerry made it easy to understand them.

"Give me the goods, Detective Quick," Kerry said. "Show me what you've got."

I opened the latch on my crossbody bag. I had tried my best to tell her that my mother hadn't sent us here, but that didn't seem to matter to Kerry, which is part of the reason I like her so much.

"I know you don't go to Ditchley, young man," Kerry said to Booker. "Are you helping with a school project here?"

"It started as a school experiment," he said, "but now we're trying to restore something valuable to its rightful owner."

"A good deed," Kerry said. "That's my favorite kind of work to do, not that it happens very often in a DNA lab."

I handed her the emery board.

"That's a relief," she said, taking it from me and holding it by the ends. "It doesn't look like much of a weapon."

"Oh, no, ma'am," Booker said. "Nothing like that. Nobody's injured here."

"See all that red stuff?" I asked, pointing my gloved finger to the top and side of the thin board. "We were at the evidence lab in Queens yesterday. Officer Hadley took a sample of it. He'll know for sure by Monday, but he thinks it's nail polish."

"And you think I might find some scrapings under the polish, or somewhere else on this?" Kerry asked.

"I was hoping so," I said.

"I can give it a try," Kerry said.

"So, I know a bit about DNA," Booker said.

Kerry smiled. "From TV shows or your science teacher?"

Booker laughed. "A mix of both, and I have some questions for you."

"Go for it."

"Suppose Dev is right," Booker said. "Suppose the woman who used the nail file—we think it's a woman, and Dev found it in her bathroom—just suppose you find her DNA on the file."

"Yeah?"

"Will that tell you anything?" Booker asked.

"Good question. I like it when one of the partners is practical."

Booker winked at me.

"I can usually develop a DNA profile from a small amount of trace evidence—in this case, from skin cells that probably rubbed off on the rough material of the emery board," Kerry said. "Now, the profile won't tell me the person's name or identify her to me. It's just a DNA profile that no one else on the entire planet has, except for that person."

"So what good does it do us?" Booker asked.

"Maybe Dev can ask the owner of the emery board to give you a sample, like a Q-tip swab of her mouth."

"Oh no," I said. "We can't do that. I'm not ready to alert her that we're looking at her. I mean, I don't want her claiming something valuable if it isn't hers."

"Are there any other ways to match her profile?" Booker asked.

"Have you learned about the databank yet?" Kerry said.

"I've heard of it," Booker said, "but I don't exactly know what it is."

My mother had explained it to me so many times that I probably could have helped Booker out here, but that would have been kind of obnoxious to do, considering Kerry was an expert in this work. I zipped my mouth.

"So there's a computer system that law enforcement all over the country uses," Kerry said, "and we call it a DNA databank.

"Suppose a person, any person, committed a crime," Kerry said. "Nothing violent, but just something that might leave evidence behind at the crime scene."

"Like if somebody broke into your grandmother's house, took a sip of her lemonade from a drinking glass, and left it in the sink," I added.

"Exactly, Dev," Kerry said. "The police might take that drinking glass as evidence, and find the person's DNA from the spot where the burglar put the glass to his or her mouth."

"Yeah," Booker said. "There's DNA in our saliva."

"So drinking glasses are good evidence," Kerry continued. "Often when we touch things, our skin cells—every one of which has DNA in it—come off on the surface that we touch."

"Then what happens to the drinking glass, for example?" Booker asked.

"The police take that glass to the local lab, and someone like me develops a DNA profile. If they have no idea who stole the sip of lemonade," Kerry said with a smile, "then they would put that profile—without knowing who it belongs to—in the national databank."

"Where there are already thousands and thousands of DNA profiles," I said.

"Exactly," Kerry said. "And then the computer takes over from detectives and from biologists like me."

"Oh, I see. The computer tries to match the DNA profile to another person already in the databank," Booker said.

"You bet," Kerry said, "and that computer search just takes hours, instead of weeks of detective work.

It might find that serial lemonade sipper anywhere."

"So there are profiles in the databank," Booker said, "that don't have any names attached to them when they are entered?"

"That's right," Kerry said. "They're just evidence found at a crime scene that may, or may not, turn out to be an important clue, and that may, or may not, be linked to a real person at some point in time."

"But there is also DNA from criminals in your system," I said. "Isn't that true?"

"From bad guys all over America," Kerry said. "If they've been arrested for crimes in some states, or found guilty in others, you can bet their profiles are in the law enforcement databank."

"Okay," Booker said. "This is coming together for me."

My phone buzzed. It was another text from Sam Cody. "All good at hospital. Going to City Hall. You and Booker cool?"

"Totally," I texted back. "Totally cool."

"Is that all you've got?" Kerry asked, waving the emery board at me.

"Actually," I said, opening my bag again, "the real deal is in here."

I fumbled with the bag's catch because of the vinyl gloves Kerry had given me, but came out with the torn paper bag and our coin.

"Way to go, Dev!" Kerry said. "Is that Olympic gold, for your swimming?"

Booker laughed. "Doesn't she just wish? This is a real doubloon. Actual pirate treasure."

Kerry got serious really quickly. She was turning the coin over and over in her hand.

"Looks like Isabella is wearing the same red nail polish that's on the emery board," Kerry said. "Where did you find this?"

"On Martha's Vineyard," Booker said. "It came up in a bucket of sand we scooped from the ocean."

Kerry lowered the coin and looked me in the eye. "Your mother knows all about this, right?"

"About the rare coin and the emery board?" I asked. "She sure does."

About our visit to the DNA lab, I thought to myself, not so much.

"I mean, you can call her," I said. "She's been pretty tied up with that hostage situation this morning, but I bet she'd have time for you."

"I almost forgot about that case," Kerry said. "We're

fine without her. Just making sure she didn't want the FBI involved in this, since you found the coin in another state."

"There's a really smart sergeant on the Vineyard who's working on that, and she's going to be talking to my aunt Blaine today," Booker said. "The FBI isn't involved at all."

"Glad to hear it," Kerry said, staring at the coin again. "I'll tell you what I'm going to do, and you can follow me out to my workbench."

"Sure," I said.

"Well, first I'm going to photograph the coin and take a close-up of Isabella's face," Kerry said. "Then I'm going to remove a slice of the polish from the surface of the coin to expose what might be underneath it. And then I'm going to swab the coin for possible DNA."

"Swab it?" Booker asked.

"Yes. I'll take a cotton swab and run it over the surface of the coin, and then process it to see if I come up with anyone's DNA."

"That's awesome," Booker said. "Are you going to do it right now?"

"You two are worse than the chief of detectives," Kerry said. "Why? Because you needed the answer yesterday?"

"That would have been very useful," I said.

We followed Kerry out of her office and down the hall to the lab area. She walked us to her workbench and placed the old coin on a clean surface after wiping the area down.

She had a camera with a zoom lens and took several photographs of the front and back of the doubloon.

Then she sat down, picked up a sharp instrument, and carved a small slice of the hard polish from the surface of the coin. She lifted it up with a pair of tweezers and put it in a tiny manila envelope.

From her desk drawer, Kerry removed several cotton swabs with long wooden handles. She rubbed a swab against the bare surface of the coin, and put it aside. She repeated that step several times.

"Okay, team," Kerry said, "now I've got to get to work to see if there's a profile."

She picked up the coin, slipped it into one of the manila envelopes—giving it a clean new home—returned it to me, and told us she would give us a call when she had something to tell us. Probably Monday.

"Thanks a million for doing this," I said.

Kerry walked us to the elevator. "Next thing you're going to tell me is that I have to split the reward the lucky owner of the coin gives you with Officer Hadley," she said, tugging on the strap of my bag.

"It better be worth a lot," Booker said, "because we're running up a big list of people who've helped us."

I pressed the button and we both thanked Kerry for her lessons—in science and crime-fighting.

"Don't you do anything wrong till I see you again," Kerry said.

"Wrong?" I was puzzled. Was she talking about me not telling my mother? "Me?"

"Just joking with you, Dev," Kerry said, pointing a finger at me and laughing as the doors started to close in our faces. "You're in our DNA databank."

I stuck my foot between the door panels and forced them open again. "What? What did you just say?"

"No big deal," Kerry said.

"Not to you maybe," I said. "But do you mean that I'm in that computer system along with every bad guy in America?"

"She's just kidding," Booker said.

"I'm not, actually," Kerry said. "But I sure didn't mean to upset you."

"Then, then what?" I asked.

"Dev, your mom has the toughest job in this city. When the mayor appointed her to be the police commissioner, we had to take her DNA and yours, in case . . . well, in case you ever got lost or anything."

My hand was shaking so badly I could hardly hold the door back. Booker grabbed it from me and pressed his arm against it.

"But I never gave you a sample. I never—"

"Your mom did," Kerry said. "She gave us the wooden stick from a Popsicle you'd been eating, okay? No big deal. I did it myself. I took your DNA off the wooden stick that you'd licked, created a profile, and entered it in the databank so we'd always know how to find you."

"They just did it to protect you," Booker said to me. "It's a good thing."

Booker thanked Kerry again, let the doors close, and pressed the button for the lobby.

"I'm twelve years old," I said to my best friend. "No one worries that I'm going to get lost."

"You were younger when they did it. I'm sure they must have thought of everything, like you getting lost," Booker said. "Why are you so upset?"

"Because the thing they must have been most worried about—my mom and the mayor and all the top guys in the department—was that I might be kidnapped because of my mom's job," I said. "That's why they wanted to have a record of my DNA on file."

I turned to look Booker in the eye. "I didn't ever realize that until just now, and it's a pretty scary thought."

26

"Favor?" I texted to Sam.

"Anything for you, kid."

"Tell Mom that Booker and I went to see Kerry at the DNA lab. Thx."

"Smart girl. Let me tell her instead of you. Where now?"

"Going home."

"Go straight there. Do not pass GO. Do not collect $200."

I laughed at his Monopoly joke.

"What do you want to do now?" Booker asked as we rode the subway uptown.

"I just promised Sam that I'd go home," I said. "I might as well start writing my paper about the experiment. I'll have the fish scale results next Friday."

"I can't believe school starts again in two weeks," Booker said. "Summer went way too fast. You want to hit some balls with me tomorrow?"

"Sure." "We should do it late morning, before it gets too hot."

"Good idea."

"Meet you at the tennis courts in the park."

"Perfect."

We both got off the train at Eighty-Sixth Street and said good-bye. I started walking east and then I heard footsteps running up behind me.

"Just me," Booker said. "I realize you've got the doubloon in your bag, and we don't even know how many thousands of dollars it's worth yet. I figure I'd better get you home."

"No reason to worry," I said. "If I disappear, just tell them to look in the databank."

"Lighten up, Dev. If anything happens, there'll be more people looking for the gold coin than there will be for you."

"Of course you're my best friend," I said. "Who else would think that way?"

I waited for the light to change to green and started to jog across the street and south toward my apartment. "See you tomorrow," I shouted back to Booker.

I unlocked the door and let myself in. Asta was delighted to see me.

"C'mon, buddy," I said to him, scratching his wiry-haired head behind both ears, which he loved. "You can help me write my report."

I sat in front of my computer and stared at the blank screen.

I picked up my phone and texted Sam. "Home. Cross-examining Asta for practice. Very tough witness. See you guys in a bit."

Sam answered a few minutes later. "That dog knows more than he's saying. Don't quit."

Sam could always make me smile. I got to work, trying to organize my thoughts and see whether there was a logical way to tell the story of my experiment without getting into the events that started when Zee pulled up the pail with the gold coin.

I drifted between my outline for the paper and watching the YouTube video of my mother, leading the hostage team this morning in her TALK-TO-ME jacket, shouting orders through her enormous bullhorn. Sometimes, she could just be fierce.

I was on the phone with my friend Katie Cion when my mother came home—five o'clock—earlier than usual.

I heard the front door open and went running to greet her. She had walked from the elevator in her bare feet, holding her heels in her hand.

"Bad way to go to a hostage situation," she said to me, lifting the shoes over her head. "Always bring along a pair of flats in your briefcase, which I forgot to do today."

My mother liked to give me practical life rules, especially tips for women in the workplace. I could have written a book already if I'd kept track of them all.

Sam was right behind her. In addition to her briefcase, she must have a lot of homework to do, because he was carrying a load of police reports.

"Mom, I took Booker to meet Kerry O today," I said. "I told Sam to tell you."

"It's okay, darling," she said. "Nothing wrong with that. There's always something new to learn at the DNA lab. In fact, Kerry called me."

"What? She snitched on me?"

"Of course not," my mother said. "Kerry was afraid that she had scared you with the story about your DNA and the databank. She'd figured you already knew."

I bit my lip and looked away. "I'm all right with it. You know what's best for me."

"Hey, Sam," my mother called out to him as she disappeared into her bedroom. "Did you hear that? Devlin Quick just admitted that I know what's best for her."

"Breaking news, Commissioner," Sam said. "Could be the morning headline."

I followed Sam to the dining room table, where he stacked up the papers my mother had to review.

I started flipping through the case reports.

"Hands off, squirt," Sam said. "Eyes only for the commish."

"What's for me?" my mother said.

She had changed into jeans and a white T-shirt that said DITCHLEY DOLPHINS, for my swim team. She was barefoot and had scrubbed off her makeup. Now she looked completely like my mom—not the boss of all those cops.

"The case reports of every major crime in the city for the last month," Sam said. "To keep you out of the heat all weekend."

"All I can think about now is dinner," she said.

"What do you feel like eating?" Sam asked me. "I bet you don't want any fish after collecting their scales all week."

"Creepy thought. How about pasta?" I asked. "Especially if you promise not to take my fork and send it to the DNA lab after I finish eating."

"Want my advice?" Sam asked. "Just order finger food."

"Good tip, Detective Cody," I said, heading into my room to get my bag and the doubloon. Nothing could be safer than a coin with its own professional bodyguard, I thought as the three of us left the apartment to go to dinner.

When we got home, I told my mother that I was playing tennis with Booker in the morning.

"Great. Sam's picking me up at seven a.m.," she said. "I have a planning session for the United Nations General Assembly meeting next month. But it should only take a few hours. Then I thought you and I might go shopping for some new fall clothes."

"Very cool," I said.

"We could have dinner at your grandmother's apartment tomorrow night."

"Lulu? I've been missing her so much," I said. "That would be great fun."

My dad's mother was one of my favorite people on the entire planet. She was a little bit outrageous. She always told people exactly what was on her mind, for better or worse, which made it more fun than anything else to be around her.

"Good," my mother said. "I'll meet you back here at one o'clock."

I said good night to Sam and my mom while they got

to work at the dining room table, which usually served as her office. I read for a while—the classic *Black Stallion* was on my summer reading list—and I liked the story. My bag was under my pillow and Asta was curled up at my side.

Just as I was about to turn out my light, a text came in from Booker. "Can you talk?"

"Sure. Call me."

I picked the phone up on the first ring.

"I just got the weirdest message," Booker said.

I sat up straight in bed. "What? What is it?"

"It must be from Zee," he said. "It came from his dad's cell phone."

"Is he okay?" I asked. "Is he still in Oak Bluffs?"

"Yes. His dad got there last night," Booker said. "It says 'THAW COINS SURPRISE' . . ."

"Surprise what?" I asked.

"That's the whole thing," he said. "That's it. That's all there is."

"Did you call Zee to ask him?"

"He doesn't have his own phone, Dev. But when I called his dad, he sounded really angry," Booker said. "He told me Zee was asleep already. That it was after nine thirty and I shouldn't be calling."

"But did you ask your uncle about the text?"

"He told me to forget I ever saw the text," Booker finally said. "He told me he didn't want us dragging Zee into any more of our trouble. My uncle said that we were already in way over our heads."

27

"It must be an anagram," I said to Booker. "The words in Zee's text must be a coded message for us."

I turned on the flashlight app on my phone and slipped out of bed. I didn't want my mom or Sam to see any light under my door. I grabbed my notepad and a pencil from my desk and got back into bed.

"Why would Zee do that?" Booker asked.

"Because he's trying to tell us something, without his dad knowing," I said. "Only I'm not clever enough to undo the letters he did. Hold on for a minute."

I started by writing the words on a piece of paper. Then I tried to rearrange them into other words.

"I can't believe Zee's dad is mad at us," I said as I shuffled letters around in my brain. "Over our heads? I mean, we've got the Oak Bluffs police and the NYPD working on this. Zee's not involved."

"My uncle's kind of a straight arrow."

"WHAT?" I said.

"Zee's dad," Booker said, "he's really strict."

"No, I meant 'WHAT'. The word WHAT is an anagram of THAW. And there's also SCRIPT, but that uses the *T* again," I said. "This is so much harder to do than I ever imagined. We need to talk to Zee."

"Well, that's not going to happen tonight," Booker said.

"I hear you," I said. "Wait!"

"Is that another word you made, or are you asking me to hold up?"

"It's both, but holding up is more important," I said. "How about if I call your grandmother? She's been with us on this since we came home with the coin. Maybe there's a chance she can tell us what Zee was trying to do."

"Right now?" Booker asked.

"Yup. Worth a try, isn't it?"

"Do it," he said. "Then call me right back, okay?"

I hung up and speed-dialed Becca's cell. "Devlin?" she said. "Is this you? I have to tell you that this little island isn't the same without you and Booker. There's hardly anything for people to gossip about."

"That sounds boring, Becca."

"Then come on back, you two."

"We'd love that," I said. "In the meantime, I think Zee's dad is mad at us. Has he talked to you about it? Is he right there with you?"

"I've got my house all to myself," Becca said. "Zee's sound asleep, and his dad walked over to Circuit Avenue to hear some band play."

"Did he tell you that Zee sent Booker a text tonight?"

"Not a word about it," she said. "But when I was putting Zee to bed, he's the one who told me."

"Told you what?"

"Let me see," Becca said, thinking through her conversation. "Zee was upset that his daddy got mad for no reason at all. He was only trying to send a message to Booker, and you know how that child loves Booker."

"Sure thing," I said. "What message? Did he tell you what the message was?"

"No, he didn't," she said. "I didn't pay him much mind, because he said he didn't get to finish the puzzle he was sending Booker by text. I just told him he could do it in the morning—from my phone, if his daddy was still in a bad way."

"That's all?" I asked.

"Well, that, and that it was about a show."

"A show? What kind of show?"

I looked at the paper on my bed. Yes, SHOW was one of the words you could make from the jumble.

"Now I didn't ask him that," Becca said.

"Do you mean a Broadway show?"

"I just don't know," she said. "All I can tell you is that Zee was reading the *New York Times* when he saw something that made him want to write the text. That's what he was looking at."

We had a copy of today's paper in the apartment.

"Now, Devlin," Becca said, "if you've got yourself a rooster that can wake you up at the crack of dawn like Zee seems to do every day, I'll be certain he calls you. Can't this all wait until then?"

"Sure it can," I said. "I didn't mean to bother you at this hour. It's just that Booker and I didn't want to get Zee in any more trouble with his dad."

"I'll watch over him till morning," Becca said. "You get yourself some sleep, will you?"

"Yes, ma'am. Thanks a lot."

I turned off my phone, opened my door, and tiptoed out toward the kitchen, where my mother stacked the newspapers at the end of the day.

"You're not asleep yet?" my mother asked when she heard me walking around.

"Close," I said. "Just a little restless."

"Was all that chattering to Asta?" she asked.

"Booker and I were making a tennis plan for the morning," I said. That was true, as far as I went.

"You're going to need all your sleep for a match against him," Sam said.

"I know," I said. "He never gives me a break. 'Night again."

I got back on my bed, flipped on the flashlight app, and turned to the Weekend Arts section of the newspaper. I skimmed the names of the Broadway shows but nothing connected to anything that Booker and I had done with Zee.

The next page had features about art museums and special exhibits around the city.

I ran my finger up and down the side of the pages, one after another. Then I came to a stop at a huge ad at the top of the fourth page.

I kept my finger on the ad while I speed-dialed Booker's number.

"Yeah?" he said. "Did Becca tell you anything?"

"She didn't know, but she remembered that it had to do with something that Zee saw in the newspaper," I said.

My finger was shaking as I tried to keep it in place to read the ad to Booker.

"What did?"

"What Zee is trying to tell us about. There's a numismatics show at Chelsea Piers on Saturday!"

"A coin show?" Booker asked. "Are you serious? Let's hope there aren't any pirates hanging around there."

28

"Are your parents okay with this?" I asked.

Booker and I were in an Uber at nine thirty Saturday morning, going from my building to the Chelsea Piers.

"My dad thought it was cool that I had a new interest in rare coins," Booker said. "My mom's in surgery. One of the Yankees had a compound fracture of his leg last night."

Aunt Janice was an orthopedic surgeon who treated several of the city's ball teams. His dad was a neurosurgeon who actually had more regular hours than his mother.

"Mine's at some meeting about the United Nations," I said. "She just wants me home at one so we can go shopping."

Booker tugged on the leather strap of my bag. "Ask her to treat you to a new one of these," he said playfully. "I'm getting kind of sick of this pink monster."

"That will be top of our list," I said. "What happened when you tried to call Zee?"

"Becca said he'd already gone out bike riding with his dad," Booker said. "I'm pretty sure my uncle is trying to make us off-limits for the time being."

It took almost half an hour to get to the Chelsea Piers from the Upper East Side. They were a series of actual piers that had once been home to ocean liners docked in New York. Sam told me that one of them was where the *Titanic* was supposed to dock on its first voyage.

Now it was a huge area made up of all kinds of sports centers. It had a golf club with a two-story driving range hanging over the Hudson River, bowling alleys, an ice-skating rink, a gymnastics training studio, and around all of these buildings there was a private marina for yachts.

"So what are we going to do?" Booker asked me.

"You know your way around here better than I do," I said.

Both of us had been to parties that included sessions on the rock-climbing wall or the ice rinks, but Booker often came down here to hit golf balls with his dad or play soccer with guys from school. The Chelsea Piers was like a Disney World for sports activities right in Manhattan, alongside a really huge river.

"What does the ad say?" Booker asked. "That will tell us where on the piers the show is."

"It says Pier Sixty."

"Easy. It's right in the middle," Booker said, leaning forward to tell the driver. "The Sky Rink is on one side of it and the golf club is on the other."

We got out of the Uber and headed into the long covered building that was marked Pier 60. It was the length of a couple of big cruise ships, and had a parking lot for cars running right through the middle of it. Large cardboard signs on easels pointed to the numismatic show at the very tip of the long pier.

"We only have to pay for one ticket," I said, reaching into my bag for a ten-dollar bill. "One of us gets in free because I brought the ad."

"Sweet," Booker said, reaching into his pants pocket and pulling out a pair of black-rimmed reading glasses. "And I remembered to bring my fake glasses."

"Great idea," I said, smiling at him. "They make you look so mature."

We had worked on a crime at the New York Public Library and discovered that when Booker wore an ordinary pair of reading glasses, he looked so much like a scholar that everyone took him more seriously.

He turned to face me and bowed at the waist. "Booker Dibble, Master of Numismatic Sorcery."

"I'm ready for your magic, Mr. Dibble," I said. "Let's figure out what we are going to be collecting."

Booker handed the man at the door our ten dollars, and I passed him my copy of the newspaper ad. In return, he gave us two admission tickets and a program. We went in and stood off to the side to study the program.

I looked over Booker's shoulder at the floor plan.

"There are about forty booths," he said. "American coins are on one side of the floor, then European coins, then Asian medals. This could get very confusing."

"We should be looking for Spanish coins, don't you think?" I asked. "Kind of like the one we found."

"We'll have to do that," he said, "because there's unlikely to be a booth called 'Stolen Coins.'"

We browsed the cases along the way to get a feeling for what was on display. There were actually lots of kids around, most with their parents. Booker reminded me how many of his friends collected stamps or baseball cards or dead butterflies—and coins. We didn't seem out of place at all.

I stopped to look at the huge silver dollars at a booth named Liberty Coins. Some pictured Lady Liberty in flowing gowns and others had just an outline of her head. There were presidential silver dollars and great-looking American Eagles from every period of our history.

Greek and Roman coins were featured by several dealers and lots of unusual antique medals, too. But I hadn't seen a single coin from a sunken galleon.

When we got to the far end of the room, I checked the program to see how many booths were left to go.

The next one was listed as TTT COINS. The description of the business said rare and unusual antiques from around the world.

I glanced up at Booker, who was staring at the glass-encased counter in front of him. The man behind the table was tall, really tall, and looked as though he lifted weights when he wasn't showing off and selling his coins. There was a huge scar across his left cheek, like he'd been in one fight too many.

Booker nodded to me and I walked toward him.

Now I could see what Booker had noticed. The sign on the counter spelled out the full name of the company: TRAVIS THAW TREASURES.

29

"You have some really great looking old coins," Booker said. "Are you Mr. Thaw?"

"Yeah." The man answered but seemed totally uninterested in talking to two kids our age. He kept scanning the room, like he was looking for an important collector he might be expecting.

"I'm starting a collection," Booker said, adjusting the glasses on his nose as he leaned over the case. "My father's been encouraging me."

The man didn't speak.

"You really do have rare coins," Booker said. "Some of these look like they're hundreds of years old."

I picked up one of the man's business cards from the countertop.

"This says you're from Martha's Vineyard and Nantucket," I said. "Is that right?"

"I used to live on Martha's Vineyard," Thaw said. "Moved to Nantucket last year. That's why the Vineyard phone number is crossed out. Why? Do you know Nantucket?"

I had never been to Nantucket, but I knew that it was farther out in the ocean than the Vineyard. I knew that it was a very expensive place to live, so when Travis Thaw sold the Chilmark farm, he must have done well enough to buy on the fancier island.

"No, sir. I've never been, but I hear it's pretty."

"I'm into pirates," Booker said, still fiddling with his glasses. "They used to hang out on those New England islands, didn't they?"

"Have you collected any pirate treasure yet, son?" Thaw asked, ignoring the question.

"A few things," Booker said.

"Real ones, or replicas?" The coin seller was getting more interested in Booker.

"My dad only wants real coins, sir," Booker said.

"How about I show you a couple of pieces," Thaw asked, taking a key from his pocket to open the case. "I've done a lot of diving off the coast of Florida, on some of the old Spanish ships that were sunk by pirates."

"That must be amazing."

"I found some of these coins myself," Thaw said.

I was squirming with excitement. I bet he did find

them. I bet he dug up Gertie's treasure on his old family farm.

He unlocked the case, lifted the lid, and brought out a handful of small silver coins.

Booker pretended to be geekily excited. "Pieces of eight! Wow!"

"Can I interest you in some of these?" Thaw asked.

"Actually, I can't buy anything until my dad gets here."

That will be a long wait, I thought to myself, since he doesn't even know what we're up to. But it was true that Dr. Dibble was glad about Booker's new interest in numismatics, so I was okay with Booker saying that.

Travis Thaw made a sour expression.

"Could I see that big gold one?" Booker asked. "Is that a doubloon?"

Thaw's hand didn't move. "That's way too expensive for someone your age. It costs thousands and thousands of dollars," he said. "Come back when your dad arrives."

"But can't I just see it?" Booker asked.

"Not right now," Thaw said, scanning the room again.

I leaned in to look at the coin Booker wanted to see. It was just like ours—the same faces of Ferdinand and Isabella of Spain. And something else was also the same.

"How come there's red paint on some of these coins?" I asked. "What's that about?"

"You a collector also?" Thaw asked.

I didn't like his tone at all.

"Thinking about it," I said.

"Well, we'll wait for *your* dad to come, too."

That was one rude step too far. "I don't have a dad."

Thaw didn't seem to care about that. "How about your mom?"

I forced a smile at him. He'd be nothing but sorry if my mom showed up to talk to him.

"What's the red paint? It must make the coin less valuable," I said.

"It's not paint," Thaw said. "It's nail polish. And the color isn't red. It's called scarlet."

Just like the scarlet silk ribbons Lemuel Kyd gave to Gertie Thaw.

"Why is it there?"

"Once I get proof that an old coin is real," he said, "I take some nail polish and put a dab of it on the coin. Doesn't hurt the value at all. In fact, just takes a cloth and some polish remover and it's all gone. It's how my regular customers know a coin is the real thing, and not a replica."

I thought again about Jenny Thaw. Two nights ago,

in her house, she had a bottle of scarlet nail polish. What kind of connection was there between these two distant relatives who didn't seem to get along?

An older woman came to the counter, holding a magnifying glass, and sort of pushed me out of the way. She started talking to Travis Thaw.

Booker turned his back to the counter and faced me, pointing at my bag.

"Why don't you show him our coin?" he asked.

"No way," I said. "It wouldn't be smart to have some stranger look at it in the middle of a coin show, when we can't even prove who it belongs to."

"Let's show it to him, Dev."

"I can't," I said, getting agitated. "I *can't* show him."

The last thing I wanted to do was bicker with my best friend. But I didn't have to, as it turned out.

Booker was looking behind me, at someone else. His jaw opened wide but he couldn't speak.

I spun around on my heel. It was Cole Bagby, the father of one of the kids who had bullied Zee—the coin collector we met in the fish market.

"Oh, it's you again," Bagby said to Booker, then he spoke to me. "And Little Miss Manners, too. What on earth are you two doing here?"

30

"I could ask you the same thing," Booker said. "Why aren't you on Martha's Vineyard?"

"I'm a coin collector," Cole Bagby said. "I never miss one of the big shows."

"Where's Ross?" I asked.

"Just outside, in the marina," Bagby said. "This kind of thing bores him, but you should go say hello. *Revenge* is docked just on the other side of the golf range."

"You came here by your boat from Martha's Vineyard?" I asked.

"Of course. How else would I come?" he said. "We left on Thursday and cruised to the tip of Long Island, where we spent the night. Then we reached the marina yesterday, in time for dinner."

I really didn't like boastful people. No wonder Ross was a bully.

"Don't let us stop you," Booker said. "You must be here to talk to Mr. Thaw."

"Exactly right," Mr. Bagby said. "He's been my dealer for years."

"I'm just getting into this coin collecting business, Mr. Bagby," Booker said. "What are your favorite things?"

"I thought Ross might have told you," he said. "I'm all about the golden age of piracy, 1650–1730. Gold coins from that period. Sunken treasure. Secrets from the deep. By the way, did you tell Mr. Thaw about the wonderful find you made off Inkwell Beach the other day?"

Bagby was talking to Booker, while I was prodding my friend to move on.

"Um, no," I said. "How did you know?"

"Ross told me, I think. Everyone on the island seems to have heard."

"I told you," Booker said. "We should have—"

I kept walking toward the door of the exhibit. "Nobody likes an 'I told you so,'" I said.

Booker was lagging behind me. "Look, Dev. Turn around."

I didn't pay any attention.

"Mr. Bagby must be telling Thaw that we found a doubloon," Booker said.

Travis Thaw was waving his hands over his head from behind his glass-topped counter. "Kids! You two! Stop right there!"

But there were so many kids in the exhibition hall that it wasn't obvious to anyone that Thaw was talking about us.

"Better get a move on," I said to Booker.

He could outrun me in a flash, but when I looked behind me, Booker was keeping pace, making sure he was covering my back.

Travis Thaw stormed across the floor of the long room, shaking his fist in our direction.

"Now I know who you are," he yelled as people moved out of his way. "Now I know your secret after all."

I was just about to make it through the door, past the security guard, when Thaw shouted to us one more time. "The devil will get you for this! I'm not done with you yet!"

31

"Keep going," Booker said.

I had turned out of the parking lot and was running on the pathway at the side of the marina.

I was winded. I stopped to put my hands on my knees while I caught my breath.

"Travis Thaw can't chase us," I said. "He can't leave all those valuable coins unprotected to come after the two of us. And the security guard can't leave the door."

Each leg of the marina was shaped like the letter *U*, in giant size. The open-ended area fed into the Hudson River. It's how the boats came into their docks. The closed end, straight ahead of us, formed the bottom of the letter *U*. We were walking in that direction, dodging the gawkers who were looking at the big boats parked along the dock.

"Which way do we go?" I asked.

"Turn right at the end," Booker said. "We'll continue straight ahead. It leads past the entrance to the golf club, and I know we can get a cab over there."

I looked at my watch as we walked. It was only eleven thirty. With a little luck and no traffic, I could still be home by one p.m. to meet my mother.

I took out my phone and texted Sam Cody while we walked. "Too hot for tennis. Booker and I went to a coin collector's show instead."

"You're telling your mom?" Booker asked as he saw my fingers move.

"Better late than never," I said.

We had reached the archway that led past the golf club entrance and out to the next section of the marina.

When we passed from the sunlight into the shaded area, a young man blocked Booker's way and held out his arm like a stop signal.

I raised my hand to my forehead till my eyes adjusted to the change in the light to see who it was.

The guy laughed, and then I recognized him. It was Ross Bagby.

"Why are you two out of breath?" he asked. "Have you been running?"

I didn't know whether to tell him about seeing his dad and being chased by Travis Thaw. He didn't have his phone in his hand, so maybe he didn't know yet.

"I was just spooked by something on the other pier," I said. "Nothing serious."

"No worries," Ross said. "Why don't you come over to our boat? It's parked right out here. If you're at the coin show because you're interested in that stuff, my dad can tell you everything you want to know about coins when he gets back."

Booker was fast to say, "Okay." He had wanted to get on that sleek-looking boat when we first saw the Bagbys in Menemsha.

We walked past the club entrance and back into the harsh summer sunlight. The second marina looked just like the first one, with boats tucked in on both sides of it.

The smaller ones, like *Revenge*, were close to this end of the dock. The large yachts were pointed toward the Hudson River, as though they were about to sail off and away.

The rear of *Revenge* was tied up against the dock. The sun made the surface of the water sparkle, and the boat was a gleaming shiny white, trimmed in navy blue. It looked pretty swell to me, too.

"Hope you don't mind taking off your shoes," Ross said. "You can just leave them here on the dock."

Booker's loafers were off in a flash. He leaned over to hold on to the boat's railing and jumped on board after Ross did.

I kicked off my shoes, too. Booker reached out his

arm and I started walking toward him on the railing on the side of the boat.

I picked my head up when I heard a familiar voice.

"Why, mateys," a man said, stepping out of the cabin up ahead, "here you are again. Welcome aboard."

I had one foot in front of the other on the railing, wobbling as though I was on the balance beam at an Olympic tryout, when I realized it was Artie Constant.

"C'mon, missy," he said. "Step on down."

My mind flashed back to Artie Constant in the lighthouse, telling us about the Bagbys and their treasure hunt, and to his last-minute evening invitation to Becca on Illumination Night.

I was teetering as I reached for Booker's hand.

"Here, missy," Artie said. "Let me help you."

But I didn't want his help. I didn't understand why he was here. So as he elbowed Booker to get closer to me, I tried to step back toward the dock.

As I pulled away, Artie's hand caught on my cross-body bag. The strap on the bag ripped off and the bag splashed into the depths of the Hudson River.

I lost my balance altogether and fell, with a far bigger splash, into the murky water of the marina.

32

"Man overboard!" Booker screamed. "Dev! Devlin!"

I came up from my plunge under the dark water gasping for air, not certain about where I was at first or how I got here.

"Don't worry," I called out. "I'm a strong swimmer."

It seemed to me our entire adventure started with those very same words almost a week ago—at the Inkwell.

I started to swim away from *Revenge* and the looming figure of Artie Constant, toward the dock on the far side of the marina. I was grateful to be wearing just a T-shirt and shorts, without shoes. There was nothing heavy to drag me under.

"Dev!" Booker shouted. "Come back this way."

Artie Constant had grabbed a mesh net that was attached to a six-foot-long pole. But he wasn't interested in me. He was fishing for my sunken bag.

"I'll be okay," I said, swallowing a mouthful of water as I tried to talk.

"Give me that pole, Artie," Booker said. "Forget the bag. Hold it out to Devlin."

But Artie Constant didn't care about what happened to me. That was clear.

I saw Booker snatch the long pole away from Artie. He tried to stretch out far enough for me to grab onto it.

"It's no use," I said, sputtering more water. "I can't reach it."

"The tide, Dev," Ross Bagby said. "Pay attention to the tide."

Ross was right. I could feel the strong pull of the tide, which was slowly going out toward the wide path of the Hudson, beyond the docks. If I got pulled that way, I'd end up in the middle of the ocean in a matter of minutes.

"Hold on," Booker shouted, ready to dive from the dock.

"No, Booker, no! Stay up there and catch me before I get to the end of the dock," I said, almost out of breath. Shouting had exhausted me. "Throw me a life preserver."

Before I could focus and make a plan, the current threw me up against the hull of a large boat. I raised my right hand to slow myself down, but the boat's surface was so slippery at the waterline that I couldn't make myself stop.

There was only one boat left at the edge of the marina, the biggest one, before the water emptied into the great river.

I turned over and started stroking again, trying to get to my right, to the rear of the giant boat so it could block the way for me.

That's when I heard a man's voice—this time, a friendly one.

"Don't panic," the man said. "We've got you."

There were two guys between me and the Hudson, dressed in black scuba gear. They both had masks on, which gave them sort of a weird look, and the one who talked first had taken the breathing device off his mouth.

"Stay as calm as you can," he said. "We won't let anything happen to you."

One of them got on each side of me.

"Are you okay to go about twelve feet?" the first one asked. "We'll get you right to the back of our boat."

I nodded my head and began to swim with them.

I could hear Booker cheering for the three of us from the side of the dock. He had run along from *Revenge* to this end of the marina, and was jumping up and down as he shouted encouragement.

The second man in scuba gear reached the broad rear end of the boat before I did. There was a ladder hanging down into the water. He held out his hand to me and pulled me up against the rungs of the ladder, so I could grab onto one of them.

The gleaming gold letters across the back of the yacht spelled *Twilight*. It was a much more welcoming message than *Revenge*.

The second guy climbed up the ladder ahead of me, and the first one stayed behind me to make sure I had the strength to hoist myself up.

I steadied myself and put both arms on the sides of the ladder. I climbed up five rungs with a burst of energy in me and stepped off onto the deck.

My legs were unsteady. It took me a few seconds to feel secure on my feet, but I was never so happy to be out of the water.

My kind companions, now out of their masks, wrapped me in a huge towel and sat me in a deck chair while I waited for Booker to make a more dignified entrance onto the yacht.

"Thank you. Thank you," I said over and over again to each of them. "I don't think I've ever been so frightened in my life."

33

"I'm Cutter," the blond-haired scuba man said. "I'm the captain of the *Twilight*. This is Mr. Moss, the steward."

"I don't know what you guys were looking for in that black water," I said, "but I'm so happy you found me."

"We were scrubbing the algae off the hull of the boat. That's why we use scuba gear, to be able to open our eyes in all this foul water," Mr. Moss said. "We were just as surprised to see you as you were to see us."

Booker was sitting cross-legged at my feet. I guess it was a good thing that he wouldn't take his eyes off me.

"Chef Tom is whipping up some lunch for you two," Cutter said. "Would you prefer hot chocolate or cold lemonade?"

"Oh, we don't want to inconvenience you anymore," I said. "I'd really just like to go home."

"Miss Quick can't go anywhere until you send some divers down to get that bag of hers that fell in the water." It was Cole Bagby, talking to us from the dock. I was startled to look up and see him there.

Captain Cutter was over at the walkway that connected the boat to the dock. I'm sure it had a proper yachting name, but it just looked like a gangplank to me.

"Why don't you come on board and we can discuss this?" Cutter said.

Mr. Moss led us from the deck to what he called the aft salon, just a few steps up and inside the yacht. It was as beautifully decorated as my grandmother's apartment. Booker whistled when we stepped inside. Cutter told us to make ourselves comfortable on one of the sofas.

I pulled the towel tight around me and stayed as close to Booker as I could get.

Mr. Bagby came on board, followed by Artie Constant, and a man wearing a light blue uniform with a tag on it that said CHELSEA PIERS SECURITY. Ross was nowhere to be seen.

"How about it, Captain?" Mr. Bagby said. "I'm happy to pay you to dive down and find the handbag that Devlin dumped in the water."

"No, thank you," Captain Cutter said, politely but with great attitude. He had a fine Southern accent to go with the attitude. "We're not for hire."

"May we leave now?" Booker asked the captain.

"There's a very valuable coin in Ms. Quick's bag, and she's not leaving until we bring it up from the bottom of the marina," Mr. Bagby said.

"With these tides running out," Cutter said, "that bag is most likely on its way out of New York Harbor, floating to Europe by now."

"Who cares about the coin," Booker said, "as long as Dev's okay?"

Chef Tom appeared with a tray full of hot and cold drinks. As he passed them around, I grabbed an ice-cold lemonade and leaned over to Booker.

"Thanks for that thought, pal," I whispered. "Between us, don't worry about the doubloon."

"Huh? It's worth a fortune," Booker said.

"It's at home. It's under the pillow on Asta's bed."

"What?"

"I didn't think it was smart to bring it to the coin show without being able to prove who owns it. Nobody's going to get close to Asta's bed except my mom, Natasha, and me," I said. "That's his nest and he protects it like a snapping turtle. Now you know why I couldn't show it to Travis Thaw when you told me to."

"What are you two up to?" Mr. Bagby asked. "What's all this whispering?"

"I'm just trying to figure out why you're so interested in some old lost coin," I said.

"That coin you found near the pier in Oak Bluffs happens to belong to me," Mr. Bagby said. "I own the doubloon."

"What?" I said. "That can't be! We found it in the water. It was abandoned and we salvaged it."

"That doesn't make you the owner of the coin, young lady."

"Well, if you own it," Booker said, "how come you didn't report it missing?"

"I bought it online from Travis Thaw," Bagby said. "But until I told him the story of your discovery, I had no idea the coin you found was my doubloon."

"Can you prove it, sir?" the security guard asked.

"It's very unusual," Bagby said. "It's solid gold. It has a picture of a man and woman on the front of it—the king and queen of Spain—and it has a dot of bright red nail polish next to the queen's face."

"Scarlet red, to be exact," I said.

"I almost saw it, too," Artie Constant piped up, shaking his finger at us. "Only these two rascals never came back to show it to me. I could have put this whole thing to rest on Martha's Vineyard. I really tried."

"You tried so hard you even snuck into my grand-

mother's house," Booker said, "trying to find our doubloon."

It may just have been a guess, but it was a really good
one.

"Aw, Becca's been my friend longer than you've been
alive," Artie Constant said. "She would have invited me
in herself if she'd been home at the time."

"Booker," I said, turning to him and squeezing both
his arms, "you solved the burglary."

"It wasn't a burglary," Artie Constant insisted.

"Sure it was," I said. "We know the law and we can
prove it."

"Now, now. It was just a social visit," Artie insisted.
"I knocked before I went inside. I can't help it that
the lady wasn't home. Becca will never press charges
against me."

"You may be right about that," I said. "She's awfully
nice. But at least it will be her choice."

Booker was on his feet. "Captain Cutter," he said,
"please don't let this man go. He's wanted by the Oak
Bluffs Police Department."

34

"What did you do with the two coins you took from Becca's house?" I asked, thinking of the replicas that Zee had bought at the museum on Cape Cod.

"Why—why—well, I guess you got me," Artie said. "I, um, I sold them to Mr. B. here in exchange for a boat ride to New York."

"You don't need to answer her questions," Mr. Bagby said. "I'll get you a good lawyer."

"Just so you know," Booker said, "those two coins that Artie found in my grandmother's house happen to be fakes."

"Fakes?" Bagby's head bobbed back and forth between Booker and Artie Constant.

"Yes, even my eight-year-old cousin knew that," Booker said, laughing at the coin collector. "He bought them at a museum gift shop."

Artie Constant shook his head and walked to one of the leather armchairs.

"Don't get too comfortable, sir," Cutter said. "The police should be on their way."

I put my head in my hands. "What's wrong with letting the marina security handle this?" I moaned, thinking about the next phone call someone would be making to my mother. "We don't need the real police."

Booker wasn't letting Mr. Bagby off the hook. "But you've had fakes before," he said. "We read a story about you online."

I thought we had both Bagby and Constant on the ropes, and that we were about to untangle this mess.

But then I noticed a large shadow fall over the side window of the salon. A man was crossing the gangplank. When he picked his head up and opened the door, I could see that it was Travis Thaw. I could also see that he was steaming mad.

35

"Where's my doubloon?" Travis Thaw roared the question at all of us. His head almost touched the ceiling of the room.

Captain Cutter was in charge. "All right, gentlemen. This is not a pirate ship, is that clear?"

"Ross just came to tell me you were all on this yacht," Thaw said. "And Cole himself told me you kids found the coin just off the beach, back on the Vineyard."

"We did," I said. "But it isn't here."

"The girl threw it in the water," Artie Constant said.

"I did not!"

"It will cost you a pretty penny if you can't find it, missy," Thaw said to me. "It's mine."

"How can it be yours, Mr. Thaw, if it's his?" I asked, pointing at Cole Bagby.

"I bought it from you," Bagby said. "I own it now."

"You haven't finished paying for it yet," Thaw said. "You were only charged a fee to hold the coin on your credit card. It's still my coin."

I didn't know why either one of them was so stubborn about claiming it when they thought it was floating away down the Hudson. They couldn't have any idea that Asta was taking his afternoon nap on top of the doubloon while we tried to figure out who it really belonged to.

"So let's think this through," I said. "Mr. Bagby, have you ever had your hands on this coin?"

He looked at me with a puzzled expression. "No," he said. "No, I haven't."

"And you haven't paid Mr. Thaw any money yet, have you?"

"Not a dime," Bagby said. "When I saw it on his website two weeks ago and called to ask about it, he didn't even have it in his shop. The one in the photograph had already been sold to someone."

"Then how could he sell it to you?" Booker asked.

"He told me he knew where to find another one, to sell to me," Bagby said. "Those were his exact words. 'I'll find you one just like the one on my site.'"

"You mean the coin Dev and Booker found isn't

the only one in the world just like it?" Cutter asked.

"Goodness, no," Bagby said. "It's a rare thing, that old coin, but there are four or five hundred of them in the world. Some are in museums, some are in private collections. . . ."

"And some are at the bottom of a muddy river," Mr. Moss said, winking at me.

"It seems to me," Cutter said, "that you really wanted to buy a coin like that for your collection, Mr. Bagby, but you never actually did."

I poked Booker with my elbow. "So far so good. Zee's still got more rights to the doubloon than Mr. Bagby does."

I stood up and paced the room, sort of the way a prosecutor would before she begins her cross-examination.

"That leaves you, Mr. Thaw," I said. "Was Mr. Bagby telling the truth? Is it a fact that you didn't have a Ferdinand and Isabella gold piece two weeks ago, but you claim to own one today?"

Travis Thaw loomed over me. It felt like a David and Goliath kind of argument. He looked like he could crush me with his thumb.

"Why don't you sit down?" the captain said to him, probably sensing the same thing.

Travis Thaw moved to one of the smaller sofas. I felt

like I had more control when he wasn't towering over me.

"When did you start your coin business, Mr. Thaw?"

"About ten years ago," he said, "when I was twenty-five years old."

"What got you interested in coins—well, in pirate treasures in particular?" I asked.

Travis Thaw was cooperating as though he'd been ordered by a judge to show up in a court of law. I think the captain gave the room an air of great authority.

"Not a big secret to Vineyarders," Thaw said, glancing up at Artie Constant. "I inherited some fancy coins."

"You inherited them?" I asked. "From whom?"

"They sort of came down in the family over the generations."

"Well, you're certainly lucky," I said. "Was your granddaddy or your great-granddaddy a pirate?"

Artie Constant slapped his thigh. "Good one," he said to me.

"No way. We were all farmers."

"Growing coins in Chilmark? You must have been the envy of all your neighbors," I said. "That must be very rich soil."

"I don't know why I'm even answering your questions," Thaw said.

Captain Cutter spoke up. "Go on, Miss Quick. Go on."

"The pirate booty, Mr. Thaw," I said. "Where did it come from?"

"One of my relatives, way back, she met a pirate," Thaw said. "She helped him bury some of his treasure, the story goes."

"That would be Gertie Thaw," I said.

Travis Thaw looked at me and blinked. "Yes, it would. You've heard of her?"

"I have," I said. "I've also met Jenny Thaw. Is she related to you, too?"

He rubbed his large hands together and scowled. "More or less. Some way or another, although it's pretty distant."

"So, if there's a family tree," I said, holding up my arms like a treetop, "you and Jenny Thaw, who lives in Oak Bluffs, are branches way down here at the bottom of the very same tree, aren't you?"

Thaw thought for a few seconds. "You could say that."

"Mr. Thaw," I said, putting one hand to my chin, "do you have anything in writing that actually proves you own these ancient coins?"

He looked away from me, bit his lip, and finally said, "No."

"Do you have anything that proves you have more of a right to this pirate booty than your distant cousin,

Jenny Thaw?" I said. "She can trace her roots back to the same part of the Thaw family in Chilmark."

"No, no, I don't have any such thing," Thaw said, shifting around in his chair. "But I know they're mine. I just know it."

"When did you dig up the doubloon we're all here fussing about?" I said. "When did you do that?"

"Why, why, it was just a week ago, I think. Maybe last Monday."

"Back up in Chilmark?" I said. "Even though you sold your farm a year ago? Even though that property no longer belongs to you?"

Booker gave me two thumbs-up. I was pretty sure I had this thing nailed.

Travis Thaw's expression slowly changed from a sneer to a wide grin. "No, ma'am. I haven't set foot in Chilmark in over a year."

I didn't know what to do. I thought of my mother's advice, which she said every lawyer learned in school. Never ask a question you don't know the answer to.

I had just fallen into that trap. I had no idea where Travis Thaw found the doubloon, but I assumed it was on the old family farm.

"But you found the coin on Martha's Vineyard?" I asked, with no idea what his answer would be.

"I know where!" Artie Constant shouted, as all heads turned to look at him. "Tell her where, Travis. Tell her where you dug."

"I didn't think you could keep quiet about it, Artie," Thaw said, pointing at his acquaintance. "You flap your mouth too much."

The town crier is what Becca had called the lighthouse keeper.

"Where was the coin?" I asked again.

"On the Vineyard, of course," Thaw said. "On Telegraph Hill."

"Telegraph Hill," I said, completely dumbfounded. "Where's that?"

Artie Constant was practically dancing a jig. "It's where the East Chop Light is. It's the land where the lighthouse sits."

36

C aptain Cutter had all he could do to keep order in
the room. "Miss Quick, you're doing fine," he said.
"Go on."

I was all twisted in knots now, because I didn't know
the answers to anything. I was nervous and not able to
think fast enough to get the job done.

"Help me, Booker," I said.

He got to his feet and put the fake glasses on the tip
of his nose.

"What is Telegraph Hill?" he asked.

"That's for me to answer," Artie Constant said. "Back
before there were lighthouses, people would pick the
highest natural point on the land and build a tower or
a station, so they could lay undersea cables and send
wires—in our case, over to Cape Cod."

"And who owns that property the lighthouse sits
on?" Booker asked. "The Thaw family?"

"No way, no how. Never," Artie Constant said. "The Coast Guard owns the lighthouse and the state owns the plot of land around it."

"Why did you go there to dig?" I asked.

Thaw put his arms up in the air, like he was going to surrender to someone. "I might as well tell you," he said. "It's not like I didn't get caught."

"By whom?" I said.

"That woman you call my cousin," he said. "By Jenny Thaw."

"How did that happen?" Booker asked.

Travis Thaw started to tell the story. "Last year, when I sold the farm, Jenny came up to ask if there was any of Gertie's stuff left around the place. Well, we found some old dresses and such up in the loft of the sheep barn, and while we were packing them up, a slip of paper fell out of the pocket of Gertie's apron."

"With writing on it?" Booker asked. "With a treasure map?"

Too much Robert Louis Stevenson, I thought to myself. Nobody drew a map to buried treasure in real life.

"No map. Just a few words. All it said was 'I'll be back for you, girl. Meet me on Telegraph Hill,'" Thaw said.

"Lemuel Kyd really did plan to return to see Gertie,"

I said to Booker, practically losing myself in a swoon at the thought of it.

"Skip the romance," Booker said. "We have a mystery to solve."

"There I was just the other day," Cole Bagby said, coming to life again, "trying to find my way around Menemsha Pond and your old farmhouse. It makes so much more sense that pirates would bury some of their treasure near a real harbor—like the one in Oak Bluffs—so it would be easy to get to on their way back to the southern seas."

"So you took the ferry back to the Vineyard last week, to dig for coins?" I asked Travis Thaw.

"If there were any coins left on the island, I figured that Telegraph Hill was the likely place they'd be," he said. "Our old farm was all dug out."

"When did you do the digging?" Booker asked.

"Late at night," Thaw said, "when I thought Artie would be off duty and no one would see me doing it."

"You didn't figure how much I love it up at the tippy-top of that lighthouse, did you?" Artie said. "Plenty of nights I sleep up there, just looking for ships at sea. It's not often I get a gold digger in my sights."

"What I didn't figure was that you'd go spill the beans to Jenny," Travis Thaw said. "At least, not so fast."

"You heard these kids," Artie Constant said. "Jenny has every bit as much right to that gold as you seem to think you have. I felt I had to go tell her."

"You mean, Jenny knows what you did at the lighthouse last week?" I asked.

"Knows?!" Travis Thaw roared. "Jenny got up there just about as soon as I found the coins. It was like Artie had lit a fire under her, she was so mad at me."

"Coins?" I said. "More than one coin?"

"Do you know what a tea caddy is, Miss Quick?" Thaw asked.

"They're old wooden boxes," I said, thinking of the one that Lulu has at home. "Small ones. It's what English people used to keep their fancy tea in."

"Well," Travis said, "I had a small garden shovel, and I was figuring there was a chance nobody else knew about the Telegraph Hill message from Kyd to Gertie. I dug holes all over the small park around the lighthouse."

"You sure did," Artie Constant said. "I filled them in the next day, telling everybody they were made by chipmunks."

"All of a sudden, I hear this dull thud," Thaw said.

"Your shovel hit the tea caddy," Booker said.

"Exactly that."

"And inside were the gold coins," Booker said. "Two of them? Three?"

Travis Thaw stopped for a few moments. "I couldn't believe it myself," he said. "I lifted the dark wooden box out of the ground and opened it up. Inside, there was an old rag, all worn and weathered from rain that had seeped in over the years."

He paused again.

"I unwrapped the rag, and there they were," Thaw said. "Gold doubloons. Coins no one had seen in more than a century."

"How many?" Booker asked again.

"Nine in all."

"Nine?" I said. There had only been one in our bucket of sand.

"That's when Jenny appeared," Thaw said. "I was on my knees, counting doubloons. There was a full moon that night—a supermoon in fact—big and bright and orange."

"Did she take you by surprise?" I asked.

"I nearly exploded from fright," Thaw said. "I didn't hear her coming up. She must have been watching me since Artie gave her the news. Jenny was standing over me, with a long broomstick in her hands, like she was about ready to lop off my head."

"But you knew it was Jenny?" I asked. "You knew it was Jenny Thaw?"

"To tell you the truth, Miss Quick," Travis Thaw said, "with a box of pirate booty and a shiny bright orange moon overhead and a broomstick that could have knocked me off my knees—I thought I'd come face-to-face with a witch."

37

"Did she hit you?" Booker asked.

"Not a chance," Thaw said. "I was on my feet and trying to bring her to her senses."

"About what?" I asked. "It seems to me Jenny had every reason in the world to be mad at you."

"She thought so, too," Thaw said. "So I told her we'd better take the discussion back to her cottage, before someone heard us out by the lighthouse."

"But they'd hear you arguing from her house, too," Booker said. "The neighbors can hear everything."

"There wasn't much to argue about at that point," Thaw said. "I pretty much realized I'd be lucky to get off the island with half of the gold."

"You split the pieces when you got to Jenny's house?" I asked.

"Even-steven," Thaw said.

"That's pretty hard to do with nine doubloons," I said.

Artie Constant couldn't hold still. "That's 'cause Travis here told her there were only eight pieces of gold."

"You lied to your cousin?" I said. "Even then?"

"I was just so nervous I think I got the count wrong," Thaw said. "Are you planning to tell the Oak Bluffs police about me, too?"

I was thinking this was more like a matter for the NYPD, because of all the resources they have. I didn't know how far back their files went, but they have a pretty amazing cold case squad for really old crimes that were never solved. They could certainly help Sergeant Wright.

"I'm not sure what to do about any of this yet," I said. "'Cause I can't figure out how nail polish got onto the coin we found, and whose coin it is after all."

Travis Thaw must have thought I was going soft on him. "Oh, the nail polish thing," he said, smiling a bit. "I told you about that when you were standing at my booth, inside the coin show."

"Tell me more," I said.

"Well, Jenny and I had a bit of time to kill after we got to her cottage," Thaw said. "I gave her the tea caddy and told her she could keep it."

"I saw it on her porch on Illumination Night," I said, looking at Booker and thinking that she probably had her treasure right there under her hand that very night, in the old battered box, with nowhere to hide it but in plain sight.

"Then I counted out the coins," Thaw said. "Most of them anyway. Four for each of us. One must have gotten stuck in my pocket."

"Wouldn't you just hate that, Booker?" I asked, turning away from Travis Thaw to roll my eyes. "If some nasty old piece of gold got stuck in your pocket?"

"Bummer," Booker said. "Real bummer."

"Anyway, Jenny told me she'd been following me on Facebook," Thaw said, "and she asked me what the red dots on my coins meant."

"So you told her it meant they were real, right?" I said.

"I did," Thaw said. "I mean, she was going to want to sell them to make some money, and there's no way these coins had been out of the ground since the eighteen thirties."

"Why did you have a bottle of nail polish with you?" Booker asked.

"Oh, son. I put that red mark on a coin the minute I know I've got a real one," Thaw said, practically pounding his fist on his knee. "I carry a bottle wherever I go. Say I got stopped speeding and the police searched me.

The red dot could prove it's mine. I got one right at my counter over at the show today."

I wasn't sure that Travis Thaw's thinking would hold water in a courtroom if the property wasn't his to begin with.

"Did you leave the bottle of polish with Jenny?" I asked.

"Nope," Thaw said. "But I told her she could walk over to the drugstore and get herself a bottle of 'Scarlet,' just like I did all those years I lived on the island. Wouldn't have bothered me if she wanted to sell her gold, too."

"She did that," Artie Constant said, looking at Thaw. "The very next day, after you left on the ferry. She used it on Illumination Night to put red marks on my doubloons. I figured if you did it to yours, people would believe mine were real, too."

"Whoa," I said. "Zee's museum replicas. The ones you took from Becca's while we were out for dinner."

"But they're fakes, Artie," Booker said to him.

"Nobody will know that now," Artie Constant said, grinning at Booker. "They've got red dots on them."

No wonder there was still scarlet polish dripping in the sink when Booker and I went inside Jenny Thaw's cottage. She must have accidentally knocked the little bottle over when company started to arrive. Now it would take an expert to sort out the real coins from the fakes, that's for sure.

Artie Constant was holding Travis Thaw's toes to the fire. "But you didn't get off the island without a fight," he said. "A fight with Jenny."

Travis Thaw looked just about defeated. He leaned back in his chair and sighed.

"It was on the dock at Oak Bluffs, just minutes before I was about to board the ferry," Thaw said. "On the foot passenger line, ticketed and ready to go."

"What happened?" Booker asked.

"Jenny insisted on walking with me until I got on the boat," Thaw said. "She didn't want me to have a chance to do any more digging—at least, not without her supervision."

"Can't say I blame her," Artie Constant said.

"Jenny was carrying the little tea caddy with her four coins," Thaw said. "She had it inside a beach bag with long handles."

"Why did she do that?" I asked.

"No locks on her cottage door," he said. "No hiding place. Jenny hadn't yet figured out how and where to keep her treasure, or whether to trust it to a local bank with a safe-deposit box."

Kind of like me, I guess, with the bag around my neck all this week.

"I was about to get to the ticket taker," Thaw said. "I reached in the pocket of my Windbreaker. When I pulled out the ferry ticket to hand it over, I accidentally grabbed a doubloon at the same time."

He went on. "Well, Jenny had been watching my every move. She reached out and rattled my pants pocket. That's where she'd seen me put the coins after we marked them."

"And there were four?" I asked.

"Jenny demanded that I empty my pocket, 'cause she thought this was another coin that I hadn't told her about," he said. "She reached up to grab it—"

"It *was* actually the ninth doubloon," Booker said.

"That's the one," Thaw said, "but she knocked it out of my hand. Accidentally, of course. Next thing I know, it was rolling along the dock on its edge, headed straight for the water."

In my head, I could almost hear the plop when the coin landed in the waves.

"You didn't dive in after it?" Mr. Bagby asked. "Are you crazy?"

"I had a choice to make, sir," Thaw said. "I still had four doubloons in my pocket, and I had a good chance of losing them all by diving into the water."

He wasn't wrong about that. The other four could have fallen out and been washed away.

"I felt in my pocket to make sure the four of them were still there, and I marched myself onto the ferry," Thaw said. "I never once looked back."

"But Jenny," I asked, "why didn't she dive into the water?"

"I can answer that," Artie Constant said. "Jenny Thaw don't know how to swim."

"What?" I said. "She's lived on an island surrounded by water all her life, but can't swim?"

"That girl never learned," Artie said. "She was always afraid to get in over her waist. That's how it is with some people."

I turned to look at Artie. "That's why you were so anxious to see our doubloon," I said to him. "You were looking out for it—for Jenny Thaw. You knew it had fallen off the dock, you knew about the red dot on the face of it, you knew Jenny needed to claim it before anyone else did, even though it really doesn't belong to her."

Artie Constant sat on the arm of the sofa. "I know all those things, missy," he said, "and now you know them, too."

Suddenly, Captain Cutter moved toward the door that led to the gangplank. I looked up.

There were two police officers in uniform, running toward the *Twilight* from the end of the marina.

Cutter opened the door and the policewoman spoke first.

"Have you got a Devlin Quick on board?" she asked, holding a walkie-talkie in her hand.

"That's me, Officer," I said, stepping forward.

"You okay, Miss Quick?" she asked me. She looked like she was ready to count my fingers and toes to double-check me.

"I'm fine," I said, throwing off the big towel so she could see I wasn't injured at all. "I'm just great."

The officer beamed a big smile back at me and spoke into her walkie-talkie. "We got an all clear on Kid Blue," she said. "Kid Blue is good to go."

38

"If you were just a little bit older," my grandmother said to Booker as we sat down to dinner, "I would offer you and Devlin some grog."

"Louella, please," my mother said, "there's no sense in that."

"That's the kind of week they've had, Blaine," Lulu said. "Every good pirate likes his grog, once they're of legal age."

Booker and I had gone directly to Lulu's apartment from the yacht. My mother met us there with dry clothes for me before two Major Case detectives debriefed us. She had also brought the doubloon, which I told her she'd find in Asta's bed.

My grandmother was fascinated with the gold coin, but even more fascinated with Booker's iPhone photographs of the yacht.

"Why don't you have any pictures, darling?" she said to me.

"My phone is gone," I said. "It was in that awful pink bag I had around my neck."

Lulu's cook, Bridey, came in from the kitchen just after we started to eat. "I'm sorry to disturb your dinner, Commissioner, but you're wanted on the phone."

"That will have to wait," Lulu said. No one came between Lulu and her dinner.

"But, Ma'am," Bridey said in her thick Irish brogue, "it's the governor of Massachusetts who wants to speak with Ms. Blaine."

I tossed my napkin on the table. "I can take it," I said. "It must be for me."

"Not this time," my mother said. "Stay put."

"Yes, darling," Lulu said, "why don't you tell me more about this yacht?"

"The *Twilight*?" I said. "It's the most beautiful thing I've ever seen. It's just enormous and decorated like it was an apartment in this building. There were paintings everywhere—one of them must have been a van Gogh, and—"

"Booker, is she exaggerating again?" Lulu asked.

"Not this time," he said with a laugh. "You'd be right at home on that yacht."

"Tell me about the owner," she said to me.

"The owner?" I asked. "We didn't meet him."

"Hmmm," she said. "Well, what did the crew say about him?"

"That he's really nice," Booker said. "They love working for him."

"Did they tell you whether he's married or not?"

"Oh, Lulu," I said, "I love your spirit. I'll call Cutter and ask him."

"Think of it," she said, "Becca and I could charter the *Twilight* and take you all on a cruise."

Booker shook his head. "It's not for charter, Mrs. Atwell. It's just the owner and his friends and family who use it."

"What a good friend to have," she said. "He seems to appreciate the finer things in life, and he has such a thoughtful crew."

My mother came back from the kitchen and looked really happy, for the first time all evening.

She stood next to Lulu and picked up the doubloon.

"The governor of Massachusetts has been made aware of your adventures," she said, looking from Booker to me. "And he's very grateful for your hard work and good judgment."

"I hope you held your tongue, Blaine, when he talked about their judgment," Lulu said.

"I did," my mother said, smiling at Booker. "I told him that I agreed with him."

"They're wonderfully bold, you know," Lulu added. "That's a quality I admire in young people."

"A quality," my mother said, patting my grandmother on the back, "and a challenge at the very same time."

"You both would have been so amazed by the way Dev got the answers from all those grown-ups today," Booker said. "She rocked."

I waved him off. "C'mon. I've watched my mom do it dozens of times in a real courtroom," I said. "You could probably set a broken leg, too, if you watched your mother in surgery."

"Will the governor's lawyers figure out who really owns the coins?" Booker asked.

"He assured me they will," my mother said. "And even the DNA results they get may help them figure it all out."

"Splendid," Lulu said. "What else?"

"The reason for the call tonight is quite simple. The little park that surrounds the East Chop Lighthouse is public property," my mother said, "and because the coin was found in Massachusetts territorial waters, the governor told me that he has already made his first decision."

"What is it?" I asked. "What did he say?"

"The governor is going to announce tomorrow that he would like to award the coin to—"

She paused just to tease us.

"He would like to give the coin to Ezekiel Dylem, who scooped the sand and raised the doubloon up from the water, where it had been lost or abandoned."

"Zee!" I shouted. "Go, Zee!"

Booker had his hands in the air, clapping for joy.

"Can we tell him, Aunt Blaine?" Booker asked.

"Right after dinner," she said, resuming her place.

"How thrilling," Lulu said. "You two should be quite proud of yourselves."

"Your grandmother is right," my mother said. Words I hadn't heard her say very often. "We're proud of you, too. Enormously proud."

"Thanks," I said.

"After you call Zee, we'll get Booker to his house and go home ourselves. We can throw your clothes in the washing machine and call it a day."

"You can't wash my clothes!" I practically shouted out.

"Don't give your mother orders, dear," Lulu said. "It doesn't become you."

"I'm sorry. I just meant that I'm going to send my shorts and shirt to the lab on Cape Cod," I said.

"Wouldn't that be a great end to my essay? I must have just about every fish scale from the Hudson River on my clothes."

"Flounder, catfish, perch, eels," Lulu said. "That's a revolting thought, really."

"We already know we had a Ditchley Dolphin in the water," my mother said. "I don't think we need any more fish scales."

"You know," Lulu said, talking to Booker and me, "with your help, we can plan next summer's vacation."

"Oh, Louella," my mother said, "you're getting way ahead of yourself here, just when I'm trying to calm things down."

"But suppose we can convince our friends who own this yacht—what is it, the *Twilight*?" she said. "Suppose we can convince them to cross the ocean with us. Is it big enough to do that? Could we get to Scotland on it?"

"You bet," Booker said. "I like your thinking."

"You two could do a science project and solve the mystery of Nessie," Lulu said.

"Nessie?" I asked.

"Surely you've heard of the Loch Ness Monster?" she said, grinning from ear to ear. "It's some kind of aquatic creature that's rumored to live in a huge lake in Scotland."

"Isn't she a myth?" I said.

"Well, you two can finally prove whether she exists or not," Lulu said.

"Fish scales of the Loch Ness monster," I said. "How cool would that be?"

"Myth," Booker said, "or mystery."

"Let's hope it's a mystery," I said, high-fiving him across the table. "Then you and I might be able to solve it."

ACKNOWLEDGMENTS

Sometimes you just get lucky.

I was sitting next to a very nice man at dinner one night at a friend's home, and he started talking to me about the most interesting things. His name is Jesse Ausubel, and he's an incredibly smart environmental scientist who works at the Rockefeller University in New York City.

Like me, Jesse has a home on Martha's Vineyard, and knows so much about fish and their DNA that I learn something every time I see him. Do you know anyone who has discovered a new species of animal life? Well, there's actually a deep-sea lobster named for Jesse! It's got a Latin name, but it's known as Ausubel's Mighty Clawed Lobster. Very cool.

One of the projects that Jesse talked to me about involves the study of water—water scooped out of oceans or rivers or ponds—to see what kinds of fish or birds or animals have left traces of their DNA behind. The minute I heard about it, I knew it was the kind of thing that would capture the imagination of Devlin and Booker.

Jesse also introduced me to some of his brilliant colleagues at Rockefeller University. Dr. Mark Stoeckle was extremely generous with his time and knowledge, and taught me some fascinating things about fish and DNA. Kate Stoeckle, his daughter, and her high school friend Louisa Strauss, solved a great mystery by using the DNA of fish when they were teenagers! Those two sleuths are truly the inspiration for this adventure of Devlin Quick's.